DON'T MISS ANY ANTICS OF THE MAN WITH THE PLAN,
FROM GORDON KORMAN:

SWINDLE
ZOOBREAK
FRAMED

SHOWOFF

GORDON KORMAN

Scholastic Press • New York

Library of Congress Cataloging-in-Publication Data available

ISBN 978-0-545-32059-7

10 9 8 7 6 5 4 3 2   12 13 14 15 16

Printed in the U.S.A.   23
First edition, January 2012

The text was set in ITC Century.
Book design by Elizabeth B. Parisi

For Daisy:

The job would be tougher without your help.

tHE DobERmAn'S LifE iS in gRAVe DanGEr
dRoP OuT WhILe yOu stILL caN
nO dOgGoNe jOkE

FOUR WEEKS EARLIER . . .

1

SURVIVING A SIX-WEEK SLEEPOVER WITH
THE MAN WITH THE PLAN
BY BEN SLOVAK

Rule 1: Absolutely NO PLANS (except for this plan for
having none)

Rule 2: When in doubt, REMEMBER RULE 1.

Rule 3: Non-plans that are really the same
as plans (operations, strategies, schemes,
brainstorms, plots, ploys, or tactics) are
STRICTLY FORBIDDEN.

Rule 4: No hair in bathroom sink . . .

"That one's definite," Ben concluded as they crossed the parking lot of the Cedarville Mall. "My mom's a clean freak. And no messing with Ferret Face. He gets really sensitive in warmer weather."

The small ferret's needle nose and beady eyes poked out from inside Ben's collar.

Griffin looked up from the paper just in time to sidestep a curbstone. "I thought you were psyched for me to stay at your place while my folks are away."

The Bings were on an eleven-country tour, trying to drum up interest in Mr. Bing's orchard inventions in Europe. The promise of the extended sleepover had prompted Griffin and Ben to stay in town, while many classmates — including their friends Logan and Pitch — had headed off to camp for the start of the summer.

"*I* am . . ." Ben hesitated. No one admired Griffin more than Ben. But in Cedarville, Griffin Bing was known as The Man With The Plan. And that had not always proved to be a good thing.

"But your folks aren't," Griffin concluded.

"They said yes, didn't they? My dad is totally on board. My mom . . ."

Griffin made a face. "She thinks I'm a menace."

"Of course not! It's just that — well, six weeks is a long time. She's a little stressed that something might — you know — go wrong."

"What could go wrong?" Griffin demanded.

The car horn sounded from so close behind them that both boys jumped. A large SUV roared past them and pulled up to the mall's gleaming entrance. The rear door opened and out jumped Savannah Drysdale and a hulking brown-and-black form nearly as tall as she was: Luthor, a Doberman pinscher the size of a small pony.

Savannah waved to the boys. "Hurry up, you guys. We don't want to miss anything."

Griffin and Ben scrambled after her, but fell back when Luthor's huge head swung around and issued a threatening growl. The Doberman was perfectly mild mannered and sweet — to Savannah. To the rest of the population, he was every ounce the trained attack dog he had once been.

At a safe distance, the boys followed Savannah and Luthor through the automatic sliding doors. The mall's huge atrium was jam-packed with hundreds of people, dozens of whom had brought their pets. There were dogs of all breeds and sizes — carried in their owners' arms, penned in plush carriers, or tethered at the ends of leashes. Excited barking filled the soaring space, mingled with a buzz of anticipation from the spectators. All eyes — human and canine — were on the raised dais, where a banner declared:

WELCOME, ELECTRA

GLOBAL KENNEL SOCIETY DOG SHOW

THREE-TIME CHAMPION

Ben turned to Savannah. "I thought you didn't approve of fluffing up dogs and forcing them to strut around like beauty pageant contestants."

"I don't," Savannah admitted. "Animals should be themselves, not glorified windup toys. But Electra is different. If she wins a fourth Global Kennel Society show next month, that record will stand forever! Dmitri Trebezhov called her the most perfect canine ever born."

"Who's Dmitri Trebezhov?" asked Griffin without much interest.

She stared at him. "I can't believe you've never heard of him. He's only the greatest dog trainer and handler in history!"

Ben looked around. "Which one is he?"

"He isn't *here*! Nobody's seen him in three years!" Savannah's face turned tragic. "Meeting him would be my life's dream. Everything I know about animals comes from his teachings. No one has ever been able to communicate with them better than he can."

"So what made him go from dog-whispering superstar to dog-whispering hermit?" Ben probed.

Savannah's sweeping gesture indicated the hullabaloo in the packed atrium. "Look around you. This isn't about animals; it's about greed! Mall tours, T-shirts, plush toys. Do you think Electra honestly cares that her paw prints are on cereal boxes? A handler and a dog are like soul mates. It's the purest, most beautiful relationship in the world. That's why Dmitri quit. He coached Electra to her first Best in Show, but then the moneymakers took over. Agents, managers, image consultants. Dmitri dropped out of sight three hours later."

"Sounds like a kook to me" was Griffin's opinion.

Luthor began to rumble deep in his chest. Savannah stroked him lovingly. "Ignore him, sweetie," she told the Doberman. "Griffin doesn't know what he's talking about."

A drum roll sounded in the atrium, and pink

spotlights began to dance across the empty stage. *"Ladies and gentlemen,"* came a public address announcement. *"Our guest of honor has arrived! Put your hands and paws together to welcome the greatest show dog in history, three-time Global winner, the Regal Beagle herself, Electra!"*

The ovation was deafening — a mixture of applause, cheers, and excited barking. On a sparkling rhinestone leash, the star herself trotted out into the spotlight. Griffin and Ben exchanged a look of utter bewilderment. After the huge buildup and the worshipful crowd reaction, they had expected a larger-than-life glowing canine beauty to glide in on gossamer wings. But the real Electra was kind of small, nicely groomed, and well behaved. She was white with attractive black and brown markings. Long ears, short fur.

Griffin regarded Savannah, whose eyes were riveted to the stage. Behind her, Luthor was up on his hind legs, giant paws on her shoulders, staring at Electra with what looked like approval.

"Maybe I'm missing something," Griffin said at last, "but isn't that just a dog?"

"I figured she'd at least be jumping through flaming hula hoops," Ben agreed in a whisper.

Savannah glared at him. "I pity poor Ferret Face for having to live with someone so out of touch with the animal kingdom."

Ben's shirt heaved and wriggled. "Speaking of Ferret Face, I don't think he's too happy. All this barking makes him nervous."

Griffin and Ben retreated a little way down the concourse. It was a good idea, since the crowd became even louder when Electra stepped up onto a platform and posed for photographs. Cameras and cell phones clicked and flashed.

A very tall woman with flaming red hair and a metallic silver raincoat dabbed at her eyes with a tissue. "She's *so* beautiful!" She held a camera but was too overcome to point it at the stage.

The boys sat on a bench, shaking their heads in wonder. They were used to Savannah's great love of all animals, but these dog-show people sure knew how to make a big deal out of nothing.

Griffin removed the folded list of rules from his pocket and handed it back to its author. "Anyway," he said, "you didn't have to write all this down, because we're not going to need it. There won't be any trouble. I promised my parents, and they promised yours."

Ben still looked worried. "It's always like that. And before you know it, we're all in the middle of a *plan*."

"You don't have a plan just to have a plan," Griffin lectured. "You have one because something's gone wrong and you have to make it right. Our lives are totally fine. Better, even. School's out, no homework, and we just scored a six-week sleepover. Where's the downside?"

A noise rose above the hubbub in the atrium — a canine roar so stomach-churningly deep, so earsplittingly loud, that it could only have come from one source. Griffin and Ben looked back just in time to see Luthor soaring over spectators' heads in a single bound. He hit the dais with a titanic thump, his hindquarters knocking out one of the poles supporting the arc lights. Down came the heavy ring, the bulbs popping and shattering in a blizzard of flying glass and shooting sparks. Electra darted in terrified circles, yapping rapidly and circling her trainer, who huddled center stage in the duck-and-cover position. Mall security agents surged forward, along with audience members shocked into action by the sight of the celebrity beagle menaced by disaster.

"What's going on?" gasped several spectators.

"That big dog's attacking Electra!" someone screamed.

"Grab his leash!"

"No!" Savannah shrieked, pushing into the fray in an attempt to reach her dog. "Luthor — come down from there!"

Dozens of spectators poured up the risers, onto the stage. A forest of hands reached for Luthor's lead. The Doberman leaped, the leash whipping over their heads. The look in the former guard dog's eyes was fierce and wild.

Griffin and Ben raced onto the scene, although how they might be of any help was a mystery to both of them. The two were scared stiff of Luthor when he was at his calmest, let alone when he'd gone completely ballistic.

"Ladies and gentlemen," entreated the announcer's voice over the PA, *"please come down off the dais! It's not approved for so much weight —"*

Electra's fans ignored him. In their minds, their beloved beagle was in danger, and they had to save her. Soon there were more people on the stage than off it.

"Move it, buster!" Savannah hip-checked a two-hundred-fifty-pound security guard out of the way and bulled through the throng to her dog.

"Sweetie" — she opened her arms to accept Luthor into a nurturing embrace — "come here —"

It was too late. The wooden stage buckled under the load of so many bodies. It split across the middle, sending people sliding down to the floor. Those who refused to slide hung on for dear life, creating a total collapse at the center. Luthor clamped his jaws around Savannah's belt and lugged her to safety.

Screams came from the melee they left behind — screams and one prize-worthy yelp.

2

MALL BRAWL PUMMELS PRIZE POOCH

CEDARVILLE, NY — A stage collapsed at Long Island's Cedarville Mall on Saturday, injuring 23 spectators and Electra, the most celebrated show dog in the world. The five-year-old beagle suffered multiple bruises, lacerations, and a tail out of joint between the sixth and seventh vertebrae.

Electra will recover, veterinarians say, but not in time to defend her title at the Global Kennel Society competition in New York City next month. The beagle was heavily favored to win an unprecedented fourth "Best in Show," the contest's highest honor, which would

have cemented her reputation as the greatest ever. That dream now lies in the wreckage of the stage, which was set up for a public appearance by Electra to promote the upcoming New York show.

The beagle became trapped in the rubble when the platform buckled after an unidentified dog stormed the rostrum.

"It was all because of this other mutt — the big one," said a mall security agent, who asked that his name be withheld. He described the canine intruder as ". . . a real monster, out to destroy everything in its path."

Ben put down the newspaper. "Do you think Luthor was really trying to attack Electra?"

"No way," Griffin said firmly. "If he wanted to get to the beagle, she'd be a grease spot right now. Nothing stops Luthor."

His friend nodded. "Except Savannah. That's why this is so weird. He usually behaves when she's around."

Griffin shrugged. "Nobody's perfect, not even Savannah." Their classmate was the greatest animal expert in Cedarville, and hostess to a menagerie of pets that matched some zoos.

Mrs. Slovak, Ben's mother, appeared in the doorway, her expression serious. "Griffin, you'd better come with us. We just got a call from the police."

Griffin leaped to his feet. "There's no plan, I swear!"

Mr. Slovak appeared behind his wife. "It's nothing like that. The alarm company reported a signal from your home. The police will be meeting us there."

Ben looked worried. "A robbery?" Ferret Face peered out of Ben's T-shirt, adding a nervous look to the mix.

"That's what we're going to find out," Mr. Slovak replied. "Let's go."

The drive was a short one, around two corners and up the street. A squad car was parked at the curb in front of the Bing house.

An upstairs window stood open, and lights blazed in every room.

"It's true, man!" Ben breathed. "Burglars must have found out your house was empty!"

"My dad's inventions!" Griffin exclaimed anxiously. He wasn't concerned about the family's possessions. Those could be replaced. But the garage was Mr. Bing's workshop. It contained a one-of-a-kind prototype for the Orchard Spritz-o-matic, Dad's latest creation. It wasn't even patented yet, which made it top secret!

As they exited the car, they heard the alarm wailing through the neighborhood. Seeing the front door open wide, Griffin began to run, but Ben's father held his arm.

"It's a crime scene," Mr. Slovak warned.

Cautiously, they approached the porch and peered into the house. The front hall was deserted.

At that moment, the alarm suddenly cut out. Now they could hear a physical struggle at the top of the stairs.

A deep voice shouted, "Come back here, you

lousy ape!" There was the pounding of running feet, followed by a loud thud.

"Gotcha!"

"They caught the guy!" hissed Griffin.

The Slovaks and Griffin stood motionless, all eyes on the stairs, waiting for the officers to bring the culprit down.

Descending footsteps. "Hold still, you little baboon!" hollered a second voice.

Mrs. Slovak wrinkled her nose disapprovingly. "You'd think our police force could make an arrest without calling people names."

The officers' shoes appeared, but there was still no sign of their arrestee. And then, there they were in the foyer — two burly policemen holding a struggling capuchin monkey between them.

"Cleopatra?" Griffin blurted, astonished.

Detective Sergeant Vizzini regarded them. "You know this — suspect?"

Griffin nodded. "It's Savannah Drysdale's monkey. What's she doing *here*?"

"I think that's pretty obvious," Vizzini rumbled. "Breaking and entering. The suspect got in through the upstairs bathroom vent and had a really good time with some talcum powder. Near as I can tell, nothing's been stolen — but you might want to count your bananas. I take it you're not pressing charges?"

"You can press charges against a monkey?" Ben asked.

"Not with us," Vizzini deadpanned. He handed Cleopatra to Griffin and turned to his fellow officer. "Make a note for the record that I'm turning the suspect over to the custody of the home owner. Now, if there are no more primates for us to arrest, we'll be on our way."

"You know, I'm kind of surprised at Savannah," Griffin commented as the squad car drove off. "It isn't like her to let her pets wander around. She's too freaked out something might happen to them."

Ben frowned at the capuchin, who was nestled against Griffin's chest, hanging on for dear life, trembling and chattering. "What's wrong with Cleopatra?"

"She's upset," Mrs. Slovak decided. "What did you expect? She's been neglected. I can't imagine what could have gotten into Savannah. If she's going to have a houseful of animals, she has to learn to take better care of them."

Griffin and Ben exchanged an uneasy glance. No one could teach Savannah anything about animal care. She already knew it all, and her pets were more important to her than her own life.

Mr. Slovak produced a cell phone and dialed the Drysdales' number. "Nobody's picking up," he announced after a moment. "They must be out."

That confirmed it for Griffin and Ben. Cleopatra was on the loose, and Savannah wasn't even home to know about it?

Something was up. Something big.

3

The Cedarville Dog Pound was located on a narrow alley off Ninth Street, just outside the downtown area. The SUV had been parked there a long time, yet no one had emerged. The passengers could not bring themselves to take that final walk to the building's front door.

Savannah sat in the rear, her arms wrapped around her beloved Luthor. "I can't do it, Dad. There must be another way."

Seated behind the wheel, her father was almost as sad, but his tone was firm. "We're being sued, Savannah — for far more money than we could ever hope to come up with. I can't even blame Electra's owners, really. They stood to make millions if their dog broke the record with a fourth Best in Show. And thanks to Luthor, that's never going to happen. That poor beagle now has a tail that wags like an organ grinder's crank."

"But they're not going to drop the lawsuit just because he's not our dog anymore," Savannah protested. "He still did what he did, and they still lose all that money."

"We've been through this a dozen times," Mrs. Drysdale said wearily. "What's done is done. We can't straighten Electra's tail. But how would it look to the judge if we didn't at least try to make sure Luthor can't harm another dog?"

"Luthor's more important than any old judge!" Savannah said tearfully.

"Is he really?" he father asked harshly. "That judge has the power to decide if we lose our home; if we can afford food, or to see doctors when we're sick; if you and your brother can go to college; if your mother and I can retire someday. We all love Luthor. *I* love Luthor. But he *is* just a dog."

Savannah pressed her face into Luthor's short coat. The big Doberman, sensing her anguish, began to whine softly.

"See how upset he is?" she sniffled. "He's sorry. I don't know what made him do such a thing."

"Yes, you do," Mrs. Drysdale said firmly. "Even you and all the love you've given him cannot overcome the guard dog training he had as a puppy. Someone made a vicious dog out of him, and that will always be a ticking time bomb inside Luthor. We can't run the risk of it going off again."

"He isn't vicious," Savannah murmured brokenly. "He's good." But even she could not explain what had happened at the mall. She was convinced that the Doberman had meant no harm to Electra. When she looked into those big, beautiful liquid-brown eyes, she saw no anger, no malice. The question remained: What had set him off?

And then there's the little matter of a 7.8-million-dollar lawsuit. . . .

"I suppose you know," she said in a strangled voice, "what happens to him if nobody adopts him."

Her parents were silent.

Savannah gave in as she'd always known she'd have to. It would take the end of the world for her to turn her back on Luthor. But this *was* the end of the world. The Drysdales were facing ruin. If there was any way she could help to prevent the coming disaster, she had to grasp at it. Her shattered heart felt that Luthor would understand.

Her father popped the locks. "Maybe you should stay in the car, sweetheart. I'll take him in."

Savannah opened the door and stepped to the

sidewalk, drawing Luthor behind her. "I'll do it, Dad," she managed bravely. "He's my responsibility. I brought him into our family, and I owe it to him not to leave his side till he's out."

The Doberman could tell something was awry, yet followed her to the door, loyal to the bitter end. Every step was a hammer blow to Savannah's heart.

I'm using his devotion against him, tricking him inside.

She had never felt lower in her life.

For a wild half-instant, she actually considered running away — not just from the pound, but from Mom and Dad, too. She and Luthor would live as fugitives. Surely Electra's owners would drop the lawsuit knowing that it had cost the Drysdales their daughter.

The insane impulse vanished as quickly as it had appeared. What would they eat? Garbage? Besides, a twelve-year-old girl with a giant Doberman would stand out like a sore thumb. The police would pick them up within hours.

She remembered the noise from when she'd first come to the Cedarville pound to adopt Luthor — the awful, discordant chorus of dogs in captivity, dogs in trouble. She introduced herself, trying not to look at the large wire-mesh kennel she knew was meant for Luthor. If she could have made the trade, she would have gladly crawled in there herself to spare her precious Doberman. This was all her fault. If she had been a better dog whisperer, maybe things would not have come to such a catastrophe.

She assisted the Humane Society attendant in gentling him into the cage. He looked at her so trustingly that her eyes welled up with tears. Maybe that was a merciful thing. She was unable to see the moment that the gate shut and he was locked in there, lost to her forever.

She hated what had happened, but not nearly as much as she hated herself.

From inside the cage, Luthor regarded her questioningly.

"His name is Luthor," she quavered, "and please be nice to him because he's the most wonderful friend anybody ever had in the whole world. . . ." She went on, but by that time, she was crying so hard that the attendant was unable to under-stand her.

It was a miracle that she made it back to the car. Sobbing now, she hurled herself into the back-seat and prepared to face life without Luthor.

On the way home, she resisted her parents' feeble attempts to comfort her. There was no comfort to be had. She had done what needed to be done for the Drysdale family. Luthor was gone and she was never going to be happy again.

"Hey," Mr. Drysdale said as they swung into their driveway. "Isn't that Estelle Slovak's car?"

Savannah sat up and peered out the window. Mrs. Slovak stood on the Drysdales' porch, accompanied by Ben and also Griffin. And what was that in Griffin's arms . . . ?

"*Cleo!*" she exclaimed, jumping from the SUV. "How did you get out of the house?"

"She *broke* out, that's how," Griffin supplied the answer. "Then she broke into *my* house and set off the alarm. It took two cops to wrestle her down."

"Something's wrong with her," Ben added, Ferret Face looking on from his collar. "I think she's upset about something."

Before Savannah could respond, the monkey bounded out of Griffin's hands, landing with a thud on the roof of the SUV. Wrapping her tail around the antenna, she hung upside down, poking her head into the open car.

The sight of her brought all Savannah's misery

crashing down upon them. "She's looking for . . . looking for . . . *Luthor*!"

"So?" Griffin was mystified by the depth of Savannah's emotions. "Everybody knows the monkey and Luthor are best friends."

"Luthor's *gone*!" she wailed.

"Gone?" echoed Ben. "Gone where?"

Eyes streaming, Savannah sobbed out the story of the 7.8-million-dollar lawsuit that had forced the Drysdales to take Luthor to the town pound.

Mrs. Slovak enfolded the distraught girl in her arms. "Savannah, I'm *so* sorry!"

The Drysdales rushed to join the group hug.

Griffin cast Ben a meaningful glance. Of course they felt terrible for their brokenhearted friend. Savannah loved all animals, but the Doberman was her favorite. She had whispered him back from the life of a guard dog, and he adored her totally and unconditionally, the way a baby loves its mother. On the other hand, a Luthor-less town was a safer town. How many times had Griffin and Ben entered the Drysdale house with a very real fear of being torn limb from limb? And the incident at the mall proved that those fears were not unfounded.

"Sorry, Savannah," Griffin told her, struggling not to sound relieved. "I know how much he meant to you."

"Yeah, that really stinks," Ben added through twisted lips.

At that moment, Cleopatra completed her search of the SUV, coming to the conclusion that her beloved best friend was gone for good. Her screech of lament was painful to the ears, and she flung herself into Savannah's embrace, chattering her sorrow.

Ferret Face burrowed deep into Ben's shirt in an attempt to escape the disturbing noise.

Savannah wrapped loving arms around the capuchin. ·"Thanks, you guys," she sniffled to Griffin and Ben. "But no matter how sad we are, we have to be strong now — for Cleo."

"We'll try," Griffin promised, hoping his friend would not notice his strangled voice.

"You're the best," she said tearfully.

It was only when the Drysdales and Cleopatra had disappeared inside the house that Griffin and Ben let out twin sighs of relief.

"Wait a minute." Mrs. Slovak wagged an accusing finger in her son's face. "You're *happy* about this?"

"I'm trying not to be," Ben defended himself.

"You're practically beaming!"

"At least we held back in front of Savannah," Griffin pointed out. "We'll get credit for that, won't we?"

"You get nothing!" Mrs. Slovak said angrily. "Your friend is devastated, and you two look like you just won the lottery."

"That dog's a killer, Mom," Ben pleaded. "He would have gotten around to me sooner or later. You and Dad would be empty nesters. Ferret Face would be back in the zoo!"

"Don't you play on my sympathies, Benjamin Slovak." His mother started for the car. "I'm disgusted with the two of you. Come on, let's go home."

As they trudged behind her, the boys looked at each other, shamefaced. There was no sin in being a little bit afraid of Luthor.

But that didn't give them the right to celebrate Savannah's tragedy.

4

"Cut it out, Ferret Face!" Griffin hissed into the dark of the room he was sharing with Ben.

For some reason, Ferret Face had taken a liking to the folding cot that was serving as Griffin's bed. The small animal was a restless sleeper, and when he rolled over, the tickle factor from his fur was almost unbearable.

But Ferret Face was part of the deal at the Slovak house. He was not a pet. He was technically a health care provider. Ben suffered from narcolepsy, which meant he could fall asleep at any time of the day. The ferret's job was to provide a wake-up nip whenever he felt his host was beginning to doze.

At night, however, Ferret Face was off duty. *Which means he's my problem for the next six weeks*, Griffin reflected with a yawn. When it came to keeping people awake, Ferret Face had a natural talent.

Griffin glanced a little resentfully at Ben, who was dead to the world. With his narcolepsy under control by day, he now slept soundly at night. He also snored — not like a buzz saw, but with just enough volume to keep a guy up. Then there was that other noise. He'd been hearing it off and on for hours. It wasn't a siren exactly, and too drawn out to be an owl. It could have been a machine that needed oiling, but who ran machines at one a.m.? An air conditioner, maybe? It wasn't that hot yet.

Restless, Griffin got out of bed, noting in annoyance that Ferret Face rolled into the middle of the cot and made himself comfortable.

I'm going to have a battle on my hands when it's time to get back in.

He opened the window a little and put his ear to the crack.

The noise was clearer now, and there was no mistaking it. It was the loneliest sound Griffin had ever heard. Howling — mournful, heartsick, suffering.

Luthor.

The Cedarville pound was more than a mile

away, but the pain in that cry was something you could almost reach out and touch. Suddenly, Griffin found himself swallowing a lump in his throat. Never before had he heard anything so sad, so desperate.

He and Ben had been scared to death of Savannah's dog, but there was nothing to fear from the source of this terrible lament. The only emotion it aroused was pure pity, and lots of it.

A wave of shame rolled over him. He and Ben had been relieved at the thought of the big Doberman confined to the pound. Pleased, even. Fine, they had sympathy for Savannah. What about Luthor himself? He was a person, too. Well, not really, but he definitely had feelings. The agonized wail that rang out all over Cedarville was the proof of that. It was nothing less than the lament of a lost soul.

A picture appeared in Griffin's mind: Luthor, drooping in a cage in the dog pound, alone and abandoned. What were the odds that someone would come along who was crazy enough, blind enough, and deaf enough to love him as much as Savannah did? What were the odds that someone would come along at all?

Who would adopt Luthor? A family with young kids? It would be like introducing a fully grown Bengal tiger into your home. And if word got around that Luthor had started the riot that had taken out the fabulous Electra . . .

Everybody knew what happened to dogs that were at the pound too long. No wonder Savannah had been crying. That had to have been in her mind when she'd left him there.

Dogs who were not adopted were put to sleep — which was a nice way of saying . . .

He couldn't even bring himself to finish the thought.

Ben was used to awakening to the feral gaze of Ferret Face. But the next morning the eyes staring down at him were human.

"Good. You're up."

There was something in Griffin's brisk, businesslike tone that made Ben nervous.

"So?" he asked with a wary yawn.

"We've got swimming at ten. We'd better hurry if we're going to make it to the dog pound before that."

Ben choked. "The dog pound? What for?"

Griffin's expression softened. "We can't leave him there."

"Yeah, we can. And we will! We've been dreaming of being rid of Luthor ever since he was the guard dog at Swindle's store."

Griffin nodded. "Not this way. If he was adopted by a family from Uzbekistan, great. I'd even buy him a carcass of raw meat to eat on the plane ride over. But if no one adopts that dog — and who would? — he's going to be put down. We can't let that happen. We owe it to Savannah. We even sort of owe it to Luthor. Horrible, vicious monsters have a right to live, too, you know."

Ben looked stricken, but he had a comeback. "Savannah loves animals more than anybody else in the world. If *she* gave up on Luthor —"

"Savannah didn't give up on Luthor," Griffin interrupted. "She was forced into it to save her family from being wiped out. You think she was happy about leaving that poor mutt on death row? She'd fall on a grenade to save a caterpillar! She's going to be scarred for life — unless we step in and bail Luthor out of the slammer."

Ben was whining now. "And do what with him? Keep him forever? Not in my house! My mother vacuums the place three times a day because of Ferret Face, and *he*'s a medical necessity!"

"It won't be your house," Griffin promised. "He can stay in our garage."

"And what are you going to tell your parents when they come back? Or are you hoping they won't notice an apex predator living in your dad's workshop?"

"That's six weeks away," Griffin scoffed.

"Lawsuits drag on for *years*!"

"Not if you settle them."

"You're talking about millions," Ben snapped back. "How's that going to happen — unless Mr. Drysdale robs a bank?"

Griffin was patient. "The lawsuit is for what Electra's owners are losing because she can't win the big dog show. So all we have to do to get exactly that much is to win it instead of Electra."

"How? We're not dogs!" His eyes widened. "Tell me you don't mean *Luthor*!"

Griffin shrugged. "Savannah always said he's big for a Doberman, but he's perfect."

"She'd think he was perfect if he had the head of a chicken and the back end of a Komodo dragon!"

"This is different," Griffin argued. "Yeah, she'd

love him no matter what. But no one knows animals better than she does. His proportions, his coat, his coloring, the way he carries himself — all ideal. That means he has a chance at the dog show. We just have to teach him to behave himself. How hard can it be?"

Ben opened his mouth to let his friend know exactly how hard it could be. At that moment, though, the stress of this argument triggered his narcolepsy, and he slumped back on the bed, fast asleep.

Instantly, Ferret Face was on the job. With a reproachful look at Griffin, he bounded onto Ben's chest, slithered underneath the pajama top, and delivered a gentle nip at his master's neck.

Ben came awake with a start, alert and ready to continue the conversation. "I know you, Griffin Bing," he said accusingly. "Don't think you're putting anything over on me. This is a *plan*."

"Maybe," Griffin admitted. "But it's also doing the right thing. Do you want that big dumb mutt on your conscience?"

5

Luthor seemed a lot less ferocious than Griffin and Ben remembered him. The Doberman was much cowed by his night at the pound. He was pathetically grateful to see two familiar faces — even if those faces belonged to Griffin and Ben, whom he'd never particularly liked. Meek and obedient, he allowed himself to be clipped onto his leash and led out of the pound.

"I can't believe it costs a hundred bucks to spring a mutt out of doggie jail," Griffin complained. "They go on TV and weep for people to adopt an unwanted animal, but when you actually try to do it, out comes the cash register. Good thing my dad left a credit card for emergencies."

"How could you just lie and say he's your dog?" Ben challenged. "What if the attendant knew the Drysdales?"

"What choice did I have?" Griffin countered. "If I told the truth, I'd have to adopt him for real, which is even more expensive, *and* I'd have to have an adult with me. Fat chance of that."

As they walked, Griffin handled the leash as if it were a brimming mug of nitroglycerin. Ben followed at a safe distance, keeping a wary eye on the Doberman.

"You know," Griffin commented after a few minutes, "this isn't as terrible as I thought it was going to be. I mean, Luthor's actually pretty calm. Maybe it won't be so hard training him for the show."

"Oh, yeah, a real breeze," Ben said sarcastically. "Since we know less than nothing about dogs, it makes perfect sense that we'll be mopping up the floor with people who've devoted their whole lives to them."

Griffin favored him with an elaborate shrug. "It's not like we have to teach him to play the piano. I did a little research on the Internet while you were sleeping last night. The contestants don't perform tricks or have special talents. All they're judged on is being dogs. Luthor's been doing that since the day he was born."

"You're dreaming," Ben said sourly. "I've seen the Global Kennel Society show on TV. They put those dogs under a microscope. They weigh them; they measure them; they examine their paws and coats and who knows what else; they shine lights into their eyes and ears. I couldn't tell you what they're looking for, but they've got to be pretty picky."

"Yeah, well, Luthor's just as good as any of those showoffs. After we check a couple of dog-training books out of the library, he's going to be *invincible*." He gazed approvingly at the Doberman at the end of the leash. "I think Savannah might have been right about him all along. Have you ever seen a more cooperative animal? He's like clay, ready to be molded by a sculptor's hands into the perfect champion."

And there, at the intersection of Honeybee Street and Park Avenue, Luthor ground to a halt and refused to move another inch.

"Come on, Luthor," Griffin wheedled. "We're going home." He tugged on the leash, but the big dog didn't budge. The Doberman sat, still as a boulder on the sidewalk, eyes obstinately fixed up Honeybee Street.

"Uh-oh." Light dawned on Ben. "To him that *is* home. Savannah's house is that way."

Griffin hesitated. To Luthor's canine mind, the

night at the pound was nothing more than some kind of misunderstanding. Why else had Griffin and Ben come to secure his release? Problem solved, he was back on the street, and it was time to go home.

But Savannah and her family were off limits until further notice.

How are we ever going to explain that to Luthor?

The answer came from Savannah herself. Animals were treated exactly the same as humans in the Drysdale home — although, in Griffin's opinion, they were treated a whole lot better. Luthor was used to being spoken to like a person.

He may not understand all the words, Savannah was fond of saying, *but he's an intelligent, sweet, sensitive creature who is more than capable of picking up the meaning.*

"Okay, Luthor, it's like this —" Griffin began, feeling foolish talking to a dog. He shrugged off a bewildered look from Ben and forged on. "You're probably all amped to go see Savannah and Cleo and the pack rat and that albino chameleon you like. And you will — soon. But in the meantime, we've hooked you up with a new place. It's just temporary. You know what I mean?"

If a dog could frown, Luthor was frowning.

"I don't think he gets it" was Ben's opinion.

Griffin opted for a simpler message. "Savannah's house — bad. Griffin's garage — good. Now let's go."

Luthor remained frozen in his tracks. Griffin drew gently on the leash, then a little harder. There was zero response from Luthor, who now appeared to be carved from stone.

"Okay, Ben. You pull, and I'll push from behind."

Ben backed off a couple of steps. "No way! He'll bite my head off!"

Griffin held out the leash. "Fine. *I'll* pull and you push."

"He'll kill you and then turn on me!"

Griffin was growing impatient. "What do you suggest we do, then? Stand in the middle of the road forever while the Drysdales get sued?"

Ben was bitter. "You promised no plans, and this one's turning into the great grandfather of them all. A million-dollar baseball card is nothing compared to entering this monster in a dog show. We can't even get him to walk down the street!"

"Well, you're the big pet owner," Griffin insisted. "Ferret Face always does what you tell him. What's your secret?"

Ben shrugged. "I bribe him. I carry pepperoni slices wherever I go. My mom goes ape over the grease stains."

Ferret Face poked his head out of Ben's collar and looked around hopefully.

"That's it!" Griffin exclaimed. "How much money have you got?"

They pooled their resources, and Ben was sent to the Cedarville McDonald's for a hamburger.

He returned in short order. "They only have breakfast. I got him an Egg McMuffin."

Luthor's nose twitched.

"Hungry?" Griffin snatched the bag from Ben and held it high in the air. "Well, right this way, sir. Breakfast is being served in my garage."

At the Bing house, Griffin punched the code on the keypad, and the garage door rattled open to reveal the organized chaos of his father's work-space. The vast tool bench and metal shop stretched across the rear. Filing cabinets bulged with schematic drawings, patent applications, and other business documents. The walls were covered with newspaper clippings singing the praises of Mr. Bing's creations — the SmartPick™, the Rollo-Bushel™, and the Vole-B-Gone™. By the wall stood the inventor's latest project, the Orchard

Spritz-o-matic. It had the appearance of a robotic garbage can, about three feet high with a rounded top and caterpillar treads, similar to those on a bulldozer. Its purpose was to wander through an orchard, bouncing off trees without damaging them, spraying fertilizer or insecticide from a ring of rotating nozzles on its "head."

"Is that your dad's new thingamajig?" asked Ben. "It looks like R2-D2."

"I wish it was," Griffin replied morosely. "At least then it would work. Dad's ready to give up on it."

He kicked a metal pail under a spigot and began to fill it with water. Luthor let out an irritated bark and snapped at the bag Griffin still held high. "Cool your jets, Ronald McDonald. You'll need something to wash that down with. Bon appétit."

He turned off the tap and tossed the breakfast bag toward the back of the workshop. It never hit the ground. Luthor was on it in an instant, snapping it out of the air and worrying the paper wrapper to get at the sandwich. Griffin and Ben hightailed it out of the garage and hit the button to close the door.

They barely made it. A split second after the weather stripping touched the driveway, a colossal crash rocked the neighborhood. Both boys stood frozen, fully expecting to see a dog-shaped hole in the segmented door and Luthor flying out at them. Luckily, the barrier held.

"Hang in there, dude," Griffin called. "We'll be back with some dog food."

Ben was pale and shaken. "What now?"

"We're late for swimming. And while we're at the community center, we'll hit the library for some dog-training books."

Another clang had the metal vibrating.

"We're going to need them," Ben prophesied.

6

"Welcome to the delightful world of show-ing purebred dogs for fun and profit. Right now, your adorable little puppy is as frisky as a March hare, a bundle of unbri-dled playfulness and love. . . ."

"No," Ben interrupted. "Right now my ador-able little puppy is trying to blast through a steel door so he can run amok and flatten Cedarville."

The two were on their way back to the Bing house. Ben struggled under a ten-pound bag of Alpo while Griffin read aloud from *Puppy Today, Champion Tomorrow*.

"If he was still doing that, we'd hear it by now," Griffin reasoned as they started up the driveway. He returned his attention to the book.

"Don't despair. Your dog may seem wild and unruly at the moment, but with the training and nurture you will learn from these pages . . ."

"You, too, can be eaten alive by a purebred Doberman," Ben finished in a nervous tone.

Griffin paused before the garage door. "He's totally calm. Not even Luthor can stay nuts forever." He punched in the code on the keypad and the opening mechanism clattered to life.

Ben tried to make himself small behind the food bag.

The metal door rose and folded out of view, revealing a scene straight from a war movie. Mr. Bing's workshop was utterly trashed. Tools were strewn from the front of the space to the back, and even the pictures and clippings from the walls had been torn down. The file cabinets lay on their sides, their contents spilled out and scattered, some of them chewed. The original SmartPick was keeled over, its long pole bent. The Rollo-Bushel had been upended, crushing the cage of the Vole-B-Gone.

Griffin's breath caught in his throat. Dad wasn't

going to be happy about the damage to his first three prototypes, but at least those inventions were completed and in production. He looked around desperately. Where was the Spritz-o-matic? It wasn't finished; it wasn't patented. Dad hadn't even gotten it to work yet!

Then he saw it. It looked as if Luthor had dribbled it like a basketball and slam-dunked it on the cement floor. The shell was dented and split open. The rounded top was off. Wires spilled out like multicolored capellini. The caterpillar treads had been torn off and dismantled, scattered all around the garage.

Luthor lay on a crumpled tarp, fast asleep, exhausted from his activities and the stress of the past twelve hours.

"I'm dead," Griffin whispered in shock. "I promised my dad I wouldn't touch his stuff."

"You didn't," Ben offered. "Luthor did."

"Same difference," Griffin breathed. "I mean, he might not kill me for the mess if I promise to cut the grass for the next fifty years. But the Spritz-o-matic — that's not done yet! He's going to have to throw it away and start over! Six months of work down the toilet, thanks to this useless mutt!"

Luthor rolled over on the tarp and began to snore.

Ben looked worried. "You're not thinking of taking him back to the dog pound, are you?"

"What do you care?" Griffin retorted savagely. "You were against this from the beginning. He scares you witless."

Ben flushed. "Yeah, but asleep he looks kind of harmless."

Griffin surveyed the wreckage. "It's when he wakes up that the trouble starts. I'm so dead."

"You know," Ben mused, "nothing's missing. Everything's still in the garage. Maybe your dad's thingy can be fixed."

Griffin reached over and tapped the guts of his father's latest invention. A tuft of tiny wires came loose and fell into his palm. "Forget it. Albert Einstein couldn't put this thing back together again."

As if in confirmation, the ring of rotating spigots fell off the robot body and toppled to the floor with a clang. The noise woke Luthor, who was on his feet and out the open door in one fluid motion.

Griffin and Ben gave frantic chase, but by the

time they were halfway down the block, the Doberman was around the corner and out of sight.

"We lost him!" wailed Ben.

Griffin slowed his pace. "Don't worry. It's not like we don't know where he's going."

Jogging now, the two loped through their neighborhood, past Ben's house and Cedarville Middle School, turning left onto Honeybee Street. By the time they reached the Drysdale home, both were sweat-drenched in the heat. But the sight that greeted them on Savannah's porch erased their exhaustion in a heartbeat.

Luthor had Melissa Dukakis pinned up against the storm door, his huge front paws pressing her shoulders into the glass. Her fearful eyes stared at the dog through the curtain of hair that usually shielded her face from the world.

"Luthor!" Griffin ordered in an authoritative tone he'd heard Savannah use. "Sit!"

The Doberman looked over his shoulder at them and growled menacingly. The boys froze on the front walk. Melissa moaned in terror.

"Don't panic," Griffin advised. "He doesn't want to hurt you. He thinks he's going home. As soon as he sees Savannah, he should be okay."

"But she's not here," Melissa quavered. "The whole family left this morning. They had to get Savannah out of town."

Ben was bewildered. "Why?"

"She was too depressed. Everything around here reminds her of Luthor."

Ben nodded nervously. "Pretty much everything in Cedarville has his teeth-marks on it."

"When are they coming back?" asked Griffin.

Melissa's stringy hair rustled in Luthor's hot breath. "Probably not till August. They're staying at some lake house their aunt owns. Mr. Drysdale brought his laptop so he can work from there. They took Cleopatra and the cats and left me the key to feed the rabbits, hamsters, turtles, mice, pack rat, and chameleon."

"The key?" Ben echoed. "What are you waiting for? Open the door, and when he runs inside, slam it real fast before he has a chance to figure out there's no Savannah."

Griffin glared at him. "Are you nuts? What if he lays waste to the place, like he did to my dad's workshop?"

"Better to trash a house than the three of us," Ben returned.

The impasse was broken by Luthor himself. The big Doberman removed a paw from Melissa, reached over, and rang the doorbell.

"She's not here, Luthor," Griffin said gently.

Luthor dropped down on all fours, releasing Melissa, who rushed over to join Griffin and Ben. The big dog stood patiently for a while, then began to pace the porch.

Griffin tried again. "Nobody's home, buddy. Sorry."

Luthor rang again, this time with his nose, and sat down to wait, whimpering a little.

Griffin pointed to the driveway. "The car's gone, too. See?"

"You realize you're talking to a dog, right?" Melissa asked.

"He's pretty smart," Griffin insisted. "Watch him — he's looking in the windows, checking the driveway. He's putting it all together. He'll figure it out."

And Luthor did. His ears drooped. His short tail lost all motion. His head went down and his belly dropped with it.

"You know," Melissa commented, "I feel really bad for him. When I first heard Savannah had to give him up, I was almost glad that he wasn't going to be around anymore. But what's he doing here? I thought he was at the dog pound."

"We sprung him," Ben admitted. "There's a plan involved."

The boys explained their strategy of turning Luthor into a prizewinning show dog in order to raise the money to cover the Drysdales' lawsuit. Melissa's eyes widened behind the curtain of hair, but she did not laugh in their faces. She was a loner who preferred the company of her computers and electronics to interaction with real people. If it hadn't been for Griffin's scheming, the brilliant girl might never have made a single friend. She had total faith in The Man With The Plan.

Ben went so far as to pat Luthor's sagging head. "Sorry, big guy. Looks like you're stuck with us."

Melissa's eyes fell on the tuft of wiring still clutched in Griffin's hand. "Where'd you get the pattern guidance circuitry?"

Griffin goggled. "You know what this is?"

"Well, not exactly. But it looks like part of the electronics that would operate a medium-sized robot."

Hope began to stir in Griffin's heart. "If I show you where it came from, do you think you could fix it?"

"I can try," Melissa offered. "What is it?"

"If my dad sees it," Griffin replied with a heavy sigh, "it's the end of the world."

7

OPERATION DOGGIE REHAB

GOAL: For Luthor to WIN the Global Kennel Society extravaganza in New York City.

Step 1: TRAIN Luthor to be just like the dogs in *Puppy Today, Champion Tomorrow.*

Step 2: WIPE UP THE COMPETITION at a smaller show as a warm-up.

Step 3: Win BEST IN SHOW at Global; give PRIZE and ENDORSEMENT MONEY to Drysdales to pay off LAWSUIT.

Step 4: RETURN Luthor to Savannah.

Step 5: FIX UP workshop in time for Dad's return.

While Melissa got down to business trying to restore the internal wiring of the broken Spritz-o-matic, Luthor's official career as a show dog began in nearby Cedarville Park.

It was a familiar place for the dog, because Savannah's house was right next door. She had taken him there almost daily for exercise and to visit the duck pond and a loon, who — along with Ferret Face — had been freed from *All Aboard Animals*, a badly run floating zoo.

"Okay," said Griffin, reading from *Puppy Today, Champion Tomorrow*. "The first thing we have to teach him is how to stack."

Ben was bewildered. "If you're going to stack dogs, don't you need more than one?"

"It doesn't mean stacking them on top of each other," Griffin said impatiently. "It's the way they have to stand to be examined and judged. If your position isn't exactly right, then your legs won't line up, or your butt will drag or be too high, or your elbow will stick out, and the judge will think you're not perfect."

"No judge is going to have to look at this dog's butt to figure out he isn't perfect. The guy's going to notice when Luthor eats the nearest pug for a pre-show snack."

"That's why you do the training," Griffin lectured. "A dog is only wild because you haven't shown him the proper way to behave. It says so right here."

A long, warbling cry came from the loon in the duck pond. Recognizing the call of an old friend, Luthor took off like a shot, galloping across the park. Long legs flailing, he hurled himself into the water with joyous abandon, drenching a woman and her toddler who were trying to feed the ducks. The flock scattered, squawking in alarm, and even the loon tried to retreat into the safety of his ruff of neck feathers.

Griffin and Ben rushed over to retrieve their pupil.

"Luthor, come back here!" ordered Griffin, and was genuinely amazed when the dog obeyed. "You see?" he said to Ben. "We're making progress."

Luthor stepped out of the pond and gave himself a good shake, spraying them from head to toe. Inside Ben's shirt, Ferret Face clucked in annoyance. He didn't like to get wet.

"Here's the deal," Griffin addressed the dog. "You have to stand with your front legs dropping straight down from your shoulders and your back legs set so that the hocks are at a right angle to the ground. No, too wide —" He reached under the Doberman to reposition the hind feet.

Luthor's head whipped around. The growl was followed by a sharp snap of dinosaur-like jaws. Griffin jumped back as if he'd been shot from a cannon.

"I don't think Luthor's too big on stacking," Ben commented.

"Yeah, well, he *has* to be," The Man With The Plan said firmly. "It's not like a beauty contest, where there's a talent competition. If he can't stack, he can't be judged. And if he can't be judged, he's out."

The two watched Luthor critically. Even when the Doberman was calm, he was in perpetual motion, always shaking a paw, or smelling the blossoms on some bushes, or digging absently in the flower beds. He was very much distracted by Savannah's house, constantly gazing into the windows, hoping to catch a glimpse of a family member. The disappointment at coming up empty was always shattering. And yet thirty seconds later, he'd be at it again, peering hopefully, only to be devastated once more.

He ran after every car that passed the Drysdale home, trampling plants and blasting through hedges, earning dirty looks from the park attendant. The man had already been forced to find a towel for the soaked mother and her toddler thanks to this unruly dog. He had no desire to redo the landscaping.

"Can a dog get ADD?" Ben mused. "My cousin has that, so my aunt cut down on his sugar intake."

"You think there's much sugar in dog food?" Griffin wondered.

Ben shrugged. "How should I know? I've never tasted it myself."

In those rare moments when Luthor slowed down or stopped, Griffin and Ben tried to compare him to the photographs in *Puppy Today, Champion Tomorrow*. According to the book, every type of dog had a "breed standard" that described the perfect animal for that breed. At a dog show, the contestants were judged on the basis of how closely they matched that ideal.

"This book stinks," Ben complained. "Where are the Doberman pictures? A fat lot of good it'll do us to compare Luthor to a championship Shih Tzu the size of Ferret Face."

Griffin pointed to another photograph. "Or this Maltese — it's so hairy you can't even tell what's supposed to be where. For all we can tell, it could have eight legs under there."

Ben frowned at the size chart. "I think Luthor's a lot bigger than a normal Doberman. What if he gets disqualified for being too big?"

"That's discrimination," Griffin said sternly. "He's perfect — see, right here."

The page showed a photograph of a prizewinning Doberman who could have been Luthor's miniature twin. If this was an example of the Doberman breed standard, then so was Luthor — just on a grander scale.

They examined their pupil, who had calmed himself long enough to provide his snout as a landing pad for a large monarch butterfly.

"You know," Ben admitted, "I thought Savannah was crazy — and you, too, for believing her. But look at him — the straight back, the way he carries himself, how he plants his feet. He's a show dog!"

"Right," said Griffin, pleased. "He just doesn't know it yet. Too bad we can't hire that butterfly on an hourly basis. Check it out — Luthor's totally stacked."

He pulled out his cell phone camera to capture

the moment. But the loon chose that very instant to emit another warbling cry.

The butterfly bailed out just in time. The stacked Doberman dissolved like a jigsaw puzzle flung into the air, its component parts just a blur. Nannies and preschoolers dove out of his path as he made a beeline for the pond. A tidal wave swamped ducks and loon.

When they finally got him out of the water again, the park attendant approached. "Look, you guys, that dog's got to go. He's too big and too wild. He's scaring the kids and scaring the ducks. And if Godzilla was here, he'd probably be scared, too."

"But he was perfectly stacked!" Griffin objected.

"I don't care if he was folded, stapled, and stuffed in a manila envelope. Take him home."

"Don't pay any attention to that guy, Luthor," Griffin grumbled as they exited through the gate. "He wouldn't know good stacking if it hit him in the head."

Luthor shook off some excess water and sneezed loudly.

"Bless you," supplied Ben.

"Anyway, we don't need this dumb park," Griffin

went on. "Better to find a place without so many distractions."

Luthor stopped suddenly, ears perked up. Down the street came a navy blue SUV. He monitored its approach and watched it pass, all aquiver. Then, with a roaring bark, he wrenched the leash out of Griffin's hand and was off in hot pursuit.

"Luthor!" cried Griffin. "Come back!"

The two boys watched in horror as Luthor flung himself at the car, clinging with all fours to the spare tire on the tailgate.

"What's he doing?" shrilled Ben. "Has he gone crazy?"

It came to Griffin. "That's the same kind of car as the Drysdales'! He thinks Savannah's in there!"

They began to run after the SUV.

"Stop, mister!" Griffin shouted.

"You've got our dog!" Ben added breathlessly.

With the athletic grace of a movie action hero, Luthor scrambled up onto the roof of the moving vehicle and clawed forward, his paws clinging to the ski rack. He reached the front and hung his head down, peering in the windshield.

It was a nasty shock for the driver of the SUV. One minute, he was navigating a quiet park-side street; the next, there was a huge, upside-down animal blocking his vision. The man did what any driver would do. He slammed on the brakes. The car screeched to a halt, flinging Luthor off the roof and over the park fence. He landed with a colossal splash dead center in the duck pond. There was a blizzard of feathers.

The park attendant was furious. "I said get him out of here, and what do you do? The exact opposite!"

"It was an accident," Griffin offered.

"How can a dog wind up in the middle of a duck pond by accident?"

Griffin and Ben exchanged an agonized look. They had an explanation — a true one, even. But who would ever believe it?

During take two of their departure from the park, Griffin had harsh words for their trainee. "Listen, Luthor, I know this has been a rough couple of days for you, but you've got to work harder. Don't you understand that we're doing all this for *you*?"

The Doberman cast a mournful glance over his shoulder at the empty Drysdale home.

"That's exactly what I'm talking about!" Griffin snapped. "You're never going to make it to the dog show if you can't get Savannah out of your head.

She's not there, and you're not going to see her anytime soon! She's gone — G-O-N-E, gone!"

Luthor let out a mournful mewl that hardened into an angry bark. He pulled back against the leash, teeth bared in a growl of open hostility.

It was behavior that Griffin and Ben remembered all too well. It came from the days before Savannah adopted Luthor.

The days when he was the toughest guard dog on Long Island.

8

"Excuse me, miss. You'll have to speak up. We must have a bad connection. There's a lot of noise on the line."

The noise was coming from the toilet, which Savannah was flushing every fifteen seconds. She was hunkered down with her father's cell phone in the bathroom of the lake house, trying not to be overheard. Her parents must not find out that she was calling the Cedarville Dog Pound.

"I'm calling to ask about Luthor, the Doberman who was dropped off last week. He's large, black and tan, and he answers to 'sweetie.' And he has the purest, most beautiful heart —"

The man cut her off. "He isn't here."

"Are you sure?" Savannah's voice rose an octave. Cleopatra reacted immediately to the tension, launching herself into the bathtub. The monkey hung from the showerhead, chattering nervously.

"I'm positive. We have no Dobermans right now."

"Did — did somebody adopt him?" she managed.

"I couldn't tell you that," came the reply. "I volunteer on Fridays, so I'm not here that often. If you leave your number, I'll have someone get back to you."

"No, thanks," she said faintly, and broke the connection. How could they call back? Dad might answer, and then he'd know she'd been asking about Luthor.

She turned to Cleopatra. "Maybe he got adopted by a good family with a big house and plenty of space to run . . ." Her voice broke, and she began to sob. In her heart of hearts, she understood that adoption was a far less likely explanation for Luthor's absence from the Cedarville pound. She knew better than anybody what happened to dogs that no one wanted.

Seeing all this, Cleopatra became so upset that she began to spin around the showerhead, squeezing the nozzle so hard that it unscrewed from the water pipe. Monkey and plumbing landed with a clank in the metal tub.

Mrs. Drysdale came rushing into the bathroom. "What's going on—" She took in the sight of the cell phone and her daughter's tear-streaked face.

"Oh, Savannah, you *didn't*!"

The girl cried harder. "I couldn't help it, Mom! And now he's not there anymore! He's *gone*!"

"Oh, honey, we talked about this! We all agreed there was no point in asking about Luthor because there was no way we could ever take him back! Not with that lawsuit hanging over us!"

"But it's just so *sad*!" Savannah wailed, devastated.

By the time Mr. Drysdale came to the bathroom to see what the ruckus was all about, he found his wife, his daughter, and the family monkey locked in a grief-stricken embrace, bawling their eyes out.

When Mrs. Slovak appeared in the doorway, Griffin quickly shoved yet another dog-training book under the bed. Ben's mom was notoriously nosy, especially when it came to The Man With The Plan.

"Telephone," she announced. But when Ben

reached for the handset, she shook her head and gave the unit to Griffin. "Your father, calling from Austria."

"Hi, Dad. How's Europe?" Griffin was a little surprised. The family had agreed to stay in touch by e-mail and Skype to save money. "Are a lot of countries going to start using Smart-Picks now?"

"It's kind of a tough sell," Mr. Bing admitted. "They like to pick fruit the old-fashioned way over here." He sounded harried. Although Dad had three patents under his belt, it was hard making a living as an inventor. "There's already a competing prod-uct to the Rollo-Bushel, and I guess voles aren't such a big deal. There seems to be some interest in the Spritz-o-matic, though. If only I could get the bugs out of it!"

"You will," Griffin assured him with a gulp. Whatever "bugs" may have been plaguing his father's latest creation, they were probably small potatoes compared with having the whole thing smashed to bits by Luthor.

Mr. Bing went on. "I don't like all this public relations stuff. I'm an idea guy, not a salesman. I should be back home in the garage finishing my invention, not shaking hands with agriculture ministers and heads of farmers' collectives."

Griffin swallowed. "Maybe it's for the best." If Mr. Bing returned to his workshop just then, he'd find no Spritz-o-matic at all. The prototype had been removed to Melissa's house in the distant hope that the electronics whiz could restore the shredded internal wiring. What Dad *would* find in his garage would be one serious mess and one seriously ill-tempered Doberman. As it sank in that Savannah was not coming back, the dog was becoming angrier and more aggressive. Any attempts to train him were met with snarly resistance. Griffin and Ben feared that, without Savannah's soothing influence, he was reverting to his old guard dog self. Griffin had already given up on *Puppy Today, Champion Tomorrow*. Now he was working from *Taming the Vicious Dog*. Hidden in Ben's sock drawer was another book from the Cedarville Public Library, *In Case of Wild Animal Attack*.

Both boys hoped they wouldn't need that one.

"You're right," Mr. Bing agreed. "This is a business, after all. And speaking of money, say hello to your mother. She has a question for you."

"Hi, Griffin. Do you have anything to tell me?"

Griffin was wary. "Everything's fine. What could there be to tell?"

"The credit card company called. Someone charged a hundred dollars at the Cedarville Dog Pound. What's that about?"

Uh-oh. "Luthor got into some trouble, Mom, and Savannah needed help. The Drysdales promise to pay you back." Okay, that was technically a lie. But he'd already resolved that the first hundred dollars of Luthor's dog show winnings would go to cover that bill.

He caught a nervous look from Ben, and flashed his friend a thumbs-up he wasn't really feeling. "Sorry, I guess I should have e-mailed you guys about that."

"As long as you're being a polite guest to the Slovaks." It was more like a question. "And you're brushing your teeth."

"I'm doing even better than that, Mom." That morning he had brushed Luthor's teeth — wearing a hockey glove, of course.

"I really miss you, sweetheart. It seems like this trip is lasting forever."

"Bye, Mom." He hung up and drew a long breath.

"There's a dog show in Garden City this weekend," he told Ben. "Technically, Luthor's not a hundred percent ready. But it's a great chance to get his feet wet and check out the kind of competition we'll run into at Global."

"Technically?" Ben's voice was thick with disbelief. "You can't take him to a dog show. In the mood he's in, he'll start a fight. And believe me, everybody else's dog is going to lose."

"That's everybody else's problem," Griffin returned stubbornly.

"Not if he gets sued again," Ben argued. "He already owes seven million bucks for what he did to Electra. Can you imagine the tab for trashing a whole show?"

"*Or,*" Griffin said pointedly, "he'll see all those other dogs stacking and gaiting and winning ribbons and he'll rise to the occasion. Cut him some slack. This was always part of the plan — a warm-up show before the big one. We're right on schedule."

"You're dreaming," Ben muttered.

"I'm not," Griffin replied seriously. "I know this isn't working out the way we'd hoped. But sometimes you just have to hold your nose and put your trust in the plan."

Ben stared at him. In the course of their friendship, Ben had put his trust in many plans, some of them disasters, all of them crazy.

He could not bring himself to put his trust in Luthor.

9

Mr. Slovak yawned wide enough to swallow the steering wheel of his car. "You couldn't pay me to jump into a cold pool at seven o'clock in the morning."

"The meet doesn't start till nine. The bus is picking us up early so we've got time to register." Ben hoped his father wouldn't notice the flush in his cheeks at the half-lie. They would be registering this morning — but not for any swim meet.

"I don't see the bus," his father remarked. "Are you boys sure you've got the right Saturday?"

"We must be the first ones here," Griffin offered brightly. Also technically true.

Mr. Slovak handed Ben an envelope. "Here's your doctor's letter about Ferret Face. They're probably not used to poolside pets."

When Ben's father drove off, the boys ducked into the bushes and changed out of their bathing suits and into the outfits they'd packed in their duffels — black shirts, black pants, and black sneakers.

"We look like undertakers," Ben complained. "Who wears black in summer?"

"Dog handlers do," Griffin replied readily. "It's in the training book. You're supposed to be invisible. That way, all the judges' attention is focused on the dog."

"In that case," Ben told him, "we should be wearing pink neon with chaser lights. The less those judges examine Luthor, the better."

They headed through the side streets to the Bing house. Griffin entered the code and both tensed for action, ready to jump out of harm's way if Luthor made his usual bull run at them. But the door rattled open to reveal the Doberman curled up on the tarp, sound asleep. He seemed to be in the midst of a good dream. A breathy, contented whine came from his massive jaws that was something close to purring.

"Think he's dreaming about Savannah?" Ben whispered.

Griffin was amazed. "I've never seen him like

this. He's almost human — you know, in a dog sort of way."

"Maybe we should let him sleep," Ben suggested.

"Are you nuts?" Gingerly, he reached down and patted the large head. "Wake up, Luthor. It's show day!"

The move nearly cost him several fingers. In a single fluid motion, Luthor rolled out of a snore into a bark, a leap, and a bone-crushing bite. Ben clamped his arms around Griffin's midsection and wrestled him out of harm's way a split second before the powerful jaws snapped shut. The two boys staggered back and toppled in a heap in a carton of spent spray-paint cans. Ferret Face appeared at Ben's collar, squeaking with outrage.

They scrambled up, ready to defend themselves, but Luthor held his ground. A strangely contented sound, not quite a growl, came from his throat.

Ben was horrified. "He's *laughing* at us!"

Griffin unzipped the duffel and took out the leash, which was buried amid packages of cookies and doggie treats. At this point, that had become their sole bargaining chip with Luthor — food.

They took advantage of the Doberman's good mood to slip on the collar and march him down to Ninth Street, past the empty shop where he had once served as a watchdog. He still growled in its direction.

A few stores past there was an auto parts supplier with a truck wash in the back. It was time for Operation Spick-and-Span. Griffin usually had total confidence in his plans, but he was a little leery about this one.

"Here goes nothing," he said to Ben.

With a nervous sigh, Ben stepped into the stall, set two handfuls of treats on the tarmac, and backed out. Griffin let go of the leash, and the Doberman went straight for the food.

"Go!" hissed Ben.

Griffin swiped his credit card and pressed the button. There was a loud click, and a deluge of ice cold soapy water poured down from above. For an instant, Luthor disappeared inside Niagara Falls.

When the spray cleared, Griffin and Ben braced themselves for his rage. What they saw instead was an oversized puppy, cowering and shivering in misery, raking them with reproachful eyes.

They gave him the second shot — the rinse cycle. The dryer was last — a powerful, sustained blast of wind that threatened to beat him into the ground. This time, Luthor howled like a soul in torment. He sounded so distressed that the boys rushed right into the teeth of the gale with their towels, wrapping him up and bringing him warmth and comfort.

"Sorry, Luthor," Griffin apologized, "but we had to do it. If we tried to give you a real bath, we'd both be dead by now."

"And — no offense — you kind of reeked before," Ben added.

Luthor actually seemed to enjoy being warmed and dried for a while. Then the primping got to be annoying, and he snarled the boys away.

Griffin checked his watch. "We're right on schedule." He picked up the leash, and the three headed to the bus stop just as the Nassau County transit pulled alongside the curb.

The driver was a little reluctant at the sight of the large guard dog in the care of two kids. "Is he well behaved?"

"Are you kidding?" Griffin answered. "We're on our way to the dog show."

"Fine. Take him to the back and keep him quiet."

Luthor was so fascinated by his first bus ride that he was completely manageable. He spent the entire trip peering at his fellow passengers with great interest. It went well until the lady sitting next to Ben began to fix her makeup. The lipstick must have had an appealing scent, because the big dog leaned over and took the end off with a single swipe of his mighty tongue. She dropped her compact, which shattered on the floor, and jumped up with a screech. The driver braked hard, knocking several people out of their seats. Fortunately, the transfer point for the Garden City bus was at the next corner. By the time the man rushed back to investigate the disturbance, Griffin, Ben, and Luthor had escaped via the back door.

The second leg of the journey passed without incident, and they got off at the campus of Garden City Community College, the venue for the Long Island Kennel Society's summer show. They could see several trailers parked in the distance. Maintenance workers were setting up a series of tents.

"I guess this is the place." Griffin turned to Luthor. "Got your game face on?"

In reply, the Doberman opened his mouth wide enough to swallow a basketball and yawned expressively.

"His back teeth are pink where he chewed the lipstick," Ben put in nervously.

"Nothing a tartar-control dog biscuit can't handle," Griffin decided. "Let's go."

10

As they approached the check-in table, they began to get a sense of how the show would run. Everything was outdoors, with three judging rings and a large "benching" area, where dogs and their owners and trainers would await their turn.

Contestants were pouring in from cars, pickup trucks, bicycle baskets, shopping carts, kiddy wagons, even a few limos. There were big dogs, small dogs, and everything in between — long hair, short hair, no hair. There were animals with so much hair that they seemed to become lost in a cocoon of it.

"Check it out," Ben whispered. "Some guy entered a sheep thinking no one will have the guts to ask what breed it is."

Griffin nodded. "And look at that one. That's not a dog; that's a blanket with legs."

Luthor was taking it all in, fascinated. Not even in the pound had he been in the company of so many other dogs. And there was another big difference. The pound was an unhappy place, resounding with angry and anxious howling and yelping. But the show dogs seemed calm and serene. There was a buzz of human conversation, but only the occasional bark from one of the contestants.

"You know," Griffin commented as they took their place in the registration line, "this may be the best idea I've ever had. Look at Luthor. He's totally into it!"

"Name?" inquired the lady behind the desk.

"Oh, hi. I'm Griffin."

"Not you. The dog."

"Right — Luthor. With an *o*."

She was patient. "That's what you call him. What is his registered name with the American Kennel Club?"

Griffin had no idea. But he wasn't going to let her know that. Reading upside down — a specialty of his — he glanced at the forms in the pile. The other contestants had official titles like *Evander Wyoming Starcatcher* and *Wilmington General Jackson III.*

"His name is Lex Luthor Savannah Spritz-o-matic," Griffin deadpanned. "Luthor for short."

He half-expected to be thrown out. The registrar simply wrote it down.

"He's a Doberman," Ben added helpfully.

"I can see that," the woman replied, "but he's awfully big. I don't recall the breed standard off the top of my head, but the average Doberman is perhaps twenty-four inches to the withers."

Griffin shrugged. "More to love."

"Yes, but I'm sure you know that a *conformation* dog show means that the contestants are judged on the basis of how they *conform* to the breed standard."

"He conforms," Griffin insisted. "Just — like — amplified."

"The judges will deduct for that," she warned.

"We'll see," Griffin replied through clenched teeth.

There were forms to sign, and the woman placed an armband with the number 11 at Griffin's elbow. Next, she handed the boys a complicated judging schedule that neither one could make out. There were hundreds of categories — several for each of the 90 different breeds represented today. Dizzying as this seemed, it was just over half of the 167 breeds recognized by the American Kennel Club. The winners of the breeds would compete for Best in Group, and those seven dogs would vie for the top prize, Best in Show.

Griffin and Ben focused on Luthor's first appointment: Dobermans, open class. 10:15 a.m. in ring two.

The benching area resembled an overcrowded outdoor baggage claim in a third-world airport. Piled around the hundreds of kennels and carriers were beat-up suitcases, bundles, and plastic bags that contained the necessities of dog show life — snacks, bottled water, hair-care products, blow-dryers, whisks, and currycombs. The owners and handlers brushed and fussed over their pets, determined to present them in the best possible condition. A few even had portable vacuum cleaners in case dust and dirt dared to fall on their dogs. Nothing could be allowed to distract the judges from the perfection of the contestant.

They found themselves a space and pulled over a couple of bales of the paper bedding used for the dog run.

Ben nudged Griffin. "Get a load of the poodle next door," he whispered. "Talk about a fuzz ball with a shaved butt!"

Griffin snickered appreciatively. "You know what's the worst thing you could do to a dog like that? Let her see herself in the mirror."

"Even Luthor can't look away," Ben added. "Man, when a fellow *dog* thinks you look dumb, it's time to find a new barber."

Yet the expression on Luthor's face wasn't curiosity, exactly. There was something more. Interest, perhaps, but also playfulness — goofiness, even. It was evident that he was aware of her, and he was trying to make her aware of him.

He strutted up and down in front of her. And when she continued to ignore him, he began to frolic about, which was no small thing when Luthor did it. The benching area was crowded, and the aisles were very narrow. It was only a matter of time before Luthor's gyrating hindquarters knocked over a tower of boxes and duffels leaning against the grooming post. A bag of dog treats spilled out onto the ground.

Luthor was onto the food like a starving shark. Amazingly, this windfall did not attract any of the well-trained show dogs in the vicinity. Even the poodle sat passively by as her food was wolfed down by this oversized neighbor.

The whole thing happened so fast that there

was nothing Griffin and Ben could do to stop it. By the time they could react, only a single dog biscuit remained. They watched, transfixed, as Luthor suddenly hesitated. Instead of swallowing the final morsel, he picked it up delicately and deposited it gently in front of the poodle. She inclined her be-frizzed head and accepted the offering in a regal manner, nibbling in a ladylike fashion. Luthor hunkered attentively at her feet.

Griffin was blown away. "That's the first time I've ever seen Luthor give up so much as a crumb to anybody else. Do you believe in love at first sight?"

"Love?" Ben stared at him. "Are you telling me that Luthor has a *crush* on that sheep-shearing accident?"

And then a voice behind them snapped, "You keep your animal away from my Jasmine!"

11

A girl about their age was storming down the makeshift aisle, expertly sidestepping water dishes and rubber bones. Griffin blinked. If they had breed standards for humans the way they did for canines, this newcomer would be a perfect example of a pretty twelve-year-old girl, right down to the finest detail — the arch of her eyebrows, the slight curl of her blond hair, the right angle of her elbows as she swooped down and scooped up her poodle, holding her protectively away from Luthor.

"Sorry," Ben began. "We tried to stop him, but he —"

Griffin silenced him with an elbow to the ribs that knocked Ferret Face out of Ben's shirt and dropped him to the grass. Terrified, the little animal disappeared up Ben's pant leg. A venue packed with dogs was not very ferret friendly.

The girl scowled at the empty bag by Luthor's front paw. "And you owe me one package of doggy treats!"

In answer, Griffin pulled a bag of s'mores out of his duffel and held it out to her.

She was horrified. "I can't feed Jasmine that! It's not right for her health! It's not right for her teeth!"

With his toe, Griffin edged the duffel behind one of the square bales until its mother lode of cookies was out of view. "It's not for Jasmine. It's for *you*," he said smoothly.

"Oh — that's okay, I guess." She accepted a s'more and took a bite. "These shows always give me low blood sugar. If I eat breakfast, I throw up, so I don't eat breakfast. I'm Emma Hightower."

"I'm Griffin and he's Ben. And you've already sort of met Luthor — at least Jasmine has. I think they like each other."

"That's another thing that's going to change," Emma declared. "Jazzy's a serious show dog. She hasn't got time for men in her life."

"Luthor's pretty serious, too," Griffin told her. "This is just a tune-up for him. He's got his sights set on the Global Kennel Society show in New York."

Emma snorted. "Him? Can he even stack?"

"Like a deck of cards," Griffin assured her.

She was dubious. "Looks like he can't sit still long enough to be judged."

"He's sitting still now," Ben pointed out.

"Only because he's all googly-eyed over Jasmine." She wagged a finger at the Doberman. "Don't even think about it, Romeo. She's in training."

It had been nearly two years since Luthor's guard dog days, but he remembered that a wagging digit was a challenge. His eyes narrowed and the short fur stood up around his collar. He snapped at the finger — missing, but not by much.

Emma jumped back, horrified. "If a judge saw that, he'd kick you so far out of this competition that you'd be swimming in Long Island Sound!"

Griffin tried to cover it up. "He's just playing with you. He's a great kidder —"

She wasn't buying it. "He was growling. He's *still* growling. He's a — a" — she goggled, barely able to finish the sentence — "a *bad dog*!"

Her words echoed like bomb blasts all around the campus. Heads turned in amazement. Even four-legged contestants sought to know the source of such a statement. In the show world, there were good dogs and better dogs. There may even have been the occasional medium dog. There were no bad dogs. Zero.

If Griffin didn't know better, he could have sworn that Jasmine was making eyes at Luthor.

At that moment, a stir rippled through the benching area. An elegantly dressed woman marched imperiously out to the parking lot, following a beautifully groomed Yorkshire terrier. The animal's silver-gray coat was so lustrous that he shone on the end of his leash.

"Who's the snoot patrol?" asked Ben, noting that the dog's nose was only slightly higher in the air than his owner's.

"That's Xerxes," Emma told him reverently. "He's the second-highest-ranked canine on the circuit today — after the great Electra, of course. You know what happened to her, right? Some terrible savage dog went wild and broke the stage at her last personal appearance."

Griffin reddened. "You don't say."

"Yeah, we heard something about that," Ben mumbled.

"Thanks to that untamed monster, Electra is out of competition. Which makes Xerxes the dog to beat now."

"I don't think that's going to be too hard," Griffin said smugly. "Look at them — they're *leaving*. They'll probably miss their judging time and get disqualified."

Emma shook her head. "Xerxes doesn't have to compete at the class level. He's a champion."

"He is?" Ben was dismayed. "Why do they bother having the dog show if they already know who wins? This whole thing is rigged!"

"Champion just means that he's earned enough points from other shows to get a 'bye' past the class level," Emma explained. "Jasmine is just four points shy of her championship. We should reach that today. Of course, dogs like Electra and Xerxes are *grand* champions."

Griffin nodded. "We were thinking of going that route with Luthor — you know, skipping over regular champion and going straight to grand."

Emma regarded him pityingly, but before she could comment, the PA system burst to life, calling the contestants in for the initial round of judging. Border collie puppies were in the first ring; the open class of Norwich terriers were in the second. American-bred standard poodles were in ring three.

"That's us, Jazzy," Emma sang out.

Jasmine followed reluctantly, tossing soulful gazes over her shoulder in Luthor's direction. Her "boyfriend" peered back, his heart in his dark eyes.

"I guess girl dogs fall for the bad boy thing, too," Ben commented.

Griffin wondered if Emma would take more notice of him if he was a bad boy — instead of just a bad dog handler.

Jasmine's departure seemed to make Luthor antsy, so the boys took him over to observe the poodle judging. They pushed their way into the crowd around ring three. There were twelve dogs of various colors, all groomed exactly like Jasmine.

"I guess the butt-shave is all the rage this year," Ben commented.

Griffin tried to seize the teachable moment for Luthor. "You see? *That*'s stacking."

The Doberman only had eyes for Jasmine, who was still as a statue, her front legs perfectly perpendicular to the ground. She might have been carved from white marble.

Griffin and Ben were waiting for the judging to begin when it was announced that the judging was over. Numbers were spoken, which meant absolutely nothing to the boys. The man might just as easily have been a quarterback calling a football play. And then a beaming Emma led Jasmine triumphantly to the winners circle.

"That must be good," Ben mused.

Everyone applauded, even the other owners and trainers. Luthor looked on with interest.

"Way to go, Emma!" Griffin cheered loudly.

It earned him a disapproving look from the winning handler.

Jasmine stood a little taller and preened.

"Come on, let's go congratulate them!" Griffin urged.

Ben was mystified. "Why?"

"They won!" Griffin insisted. "They're moving on to Best of Breed."

"What do we care about the poodle contest? We're Dobermans."

Sure enough, the next announcement called the open class of Dobermans to the second ring.

"This is it!" Griffin exclaimed excitedly.

They had always known that Luthor was large for his breed, but this was the first time they'd seen him next to other Dobermans. They barely came up to his withers, and his head towered over them. In every other way, the eleven dogs were identical — short black-and-tan fur, elegant body lines, strong and muscular, with a proud demeanor. There was a buzz around the ring as spectators discussed "the big guy," and whether or not he was a true Doberman, or perhaps interbred with Great Dane bloodlines. Ben tried to counteract this by announcing loudly, "Are you sure those little guys are the real deal? They look part Chihuahua to me!"

One of the owners, a man with a heavily waxed mustache that gave him the appearance of holding a stick in his mouth, seemed to be arguing with the judge. Griffin couldn't hear the conversation, but from the pointing and gesturing, it was clear the man was complaining about Luthor. The judge seemed to be ignoring him, but she was looking at Luthor with perhaps a touch of suspicion.

Before lining up for stacking, the smaller contestants formed a group around Luthor, as if acknowledging the king.

Griffin knew a moment of fear when the judge stepped into the ring. Luthor was nothing if not unpredictable. But as the other dogs fell into stacking position at the end of their leashes, Luthor followed suit. So far, so good.

This judge — an older woman — was all business, grim and unsmiling. At first, she walked around the ring, examining the animals from many different angles.

Hurry up, Griffin thought to himself, *you're judging, not buying a used car.*

"Take them around," she commanded.

Around what? But when the other handlers began leading the dogs around the perimeter of the ring, he fell into line. It was a little tricky, since Luthor's stride was longer than that of the competition, and soon he was tailgating. Griffin tried to pull back on the leash, but Luthor cast him a look of such annoyance that he eased off. The big Doberman was used to obstacles getting out of *his* way, not vice versa.

Fortunately, the judge restacked the class before any trampling could take place. She moved from dog to dog, examining the contestants close up. She looked into their mouths, counting teeth, and placed hands on firm bellies, checking musculature.

Uh-oh. Griffin wasn't too sure about this. Luthor was doing awesome so far, but he wasn't a hands-on kind of pooch. If the judge looked closely enough into his mouth, she was likely to get a guided tour of the inside of his stomach.

Before he knew it, the woman was headed in their direction.

"Listen, Luthor," he whispered, "some pretty bad stuff is going to happen in a minute. So just close your eyes and think of hamburgers."

Luthor was pretty good about having his mouth examined, but when the judge squeezed his haunch, he felt he had put up with enough. He sprang straight up, yanking the leash from Griffin's hand, and twisting an athletic one-eighty in mid-air. He came down facing the woman, and emitted a bark so loud and so full of indignation that she staggered backward ten feet. The noise reverberated all across the campus, bringing activity in the other two rings to an abrupt halt. Inside Ben's shirt, Ferret Face tensed in fear, chafing at his host's skin.

"Excused," panted the judge.

Griffin heaved a sigh of relief. "Phew! For a minute there, I thought we were in trouble."

She glared at him. "This dog is excused from competition."

But Luthor had already excused himself, bounding across the campus. He came down in the midst of the Pekingese breed judging, sending the furry little creatures scattering in all directions. As he cleared the gate, he upended the check-in table in a blizzard of fluttering papers. It all happened so fast that the show superintendents could do nothing but stand and watch.

"Luthor, come back!" Griffin ran as fast as he could, but an English bulldog took him out at the knees, and he hit the turf like a sack of kibble. He got up and shook himself just in time to see Emma Hightower's look of thorough disgust.

By the time he and Ben pounded out onto the street, the big Doberman had already disappeared.

12

"*L uthor!*" Griffin's voice was almost gone now, from shouting down alleys, up streets, and into backyards. "*Lu-u-u-thor!!*"

They had been searching for hours, sweat-drenched and exhausted in the afternoon heat. The Doberman was nowhere to be found.

Ben was getting cranky. "We have to give up, Griffin. Sooner or later, my parents are going to expect us to come home from swimming. If they figure out what we've got going on, we'll have bigger problems than a lost dog. We promised no plans, remember?"

"Just one more neighborhood," Griffin argued. "Luthor wouldn't even be here if it wasn't for us."

"And we wouldn't be here if it wasn't for him," Ben countered. "Did we ask him to get the Drysdales sued and land us on the professional dog show circuit? I was perfectly happy back when I thought stacking meant putting stuff on top of other stuff."

"One last street," Griffin pleaded. "Then we'll go."

Legs aching, they dragged themselves up and down a few more blocks, rasping the dog's name over failing vocal cords. No Luthor.

When they finally slogged back to the bus stop, totally defeated, the Long Island Kennel Society show was just breaking up.

"I wish we didn't have to see this," Griffin mourned. "All these people loading their dogs back into cars. It's like they're rubbing it our faces that Luthor went AWOL."

They watched as Xerxes' snooty owner walked by, nose still in the air. The triumphant Yorkshire terrier sported a blue prize ribbon that was larger than he was.

"Real impressive," Ben gritted sarcastically. "I'd like to see that hairy squirrel take on Luthor at ultimate fighting."

On the bus, they sat in stiff-necked misery, too tired and dispirited for conversation.

"When we get home," Griffin decided, "we'll call Garden City animal control. Surely somebody's picked Luthor up by now. He's not the kind of guy you overlook. Maybe they'll transfer him back to the Cedarville pound so we can bail him out again."

"I've got a better idea," Ben grumbled. "Let's not, and say we did."

Yet both knew they would not abandon Luthor to his fate. The question was what could they possibly do to save him? If the Doberman could not tolerate being handled by a judge, he would never be able to compete in a dog show, much less win the biggest one of all.

The bus let them off in front of Cedarville Auto Parts, and they started for home.

Griffin regarded the truck-wash stall with regret. "Maybe we shouldn't have put him through that thing. I think we broke his spirit."

"He seemed pretty spirited when he flattened the registration table and cleared the fence by three feet," Ben noted. "If anything's broken, it isn't his spirit."

"You're right!" A lightbulb went off in Griffin's head. He began to run.

"Where are you going?" Ben stepped up his pace and followed his friend through downtown, turning left onto Honeybee Street.

They passed the park and stopped in front of the Drysdale house.

"It's not his spirit that's broken," Griffin panted. "It's his heart. Look."

Across the doorway like a welcome mat lay an expanse of black-and-tan fur. The great head drooped across the front paws.

"At times of stress, he needs Savannah," Ben concluded.

"And he's lost her," Griffin finished.

They looked at the huge Doberman, star of so many of their nightmares. Never could they have imagined themselves capable of so much sympathy for this oversized brute.

"How are we ever going to help him?" Ben mused hopelessly.

The Man With The Plan had no answer.

They were distracted by a faint tapping sound that seemed to be coming from inside the house. Griffin squinted at the living room window. There stood a familiar figure, signaling frantically. Melissa's eyes looked haunted behind her curtain of hair.

Griffin headed for the house. "She was probably feeding the other animals when Luthor showed. I'll bet she's afraid to come out."

They rushed up the porch steps. Griffin had one last treat, which he used to coax the Doberman away from the door.

Ben sprang Melissa. "How long have you been in there?"

"Not long. Maybe an hour." Having friends was still new to shy Melissa. She was reluctant to complain. "I did some calculations in my head to pass the time."

"Calculations about the Spritz-o-matic?" Griffin asked eagerly. "Are you making any progress with that?"

"Some," she replied. "The wiring's very complicated. It'll take time. How did Luthor do at the dog show?"

"He fell in love with a puff-ball," Ben told her. "But then the judge got too personal, and Luthor hit the bricks —"

"Don't listen to Ben," Griffin interrupted. "You know what a sad sack he is. The plan is coming along perfectly."

"Well, thanks for letting me out. I'd better go. My mom's expecting me — at least, she was an hour ago."

When Melissa was gone, Ben rounded on his friend. "How can you lie like that? The plan isn't coming along perfectly! It isn't coming along at all!"

"Sure it is. Think about it: We cleaned Luthor up and got him where he had to be. And he behaved himself — until he didn't anymore. You saw those so-called champions. They were no better than our guy."

"Except that they stayed, and he jumped the fence and took off," Ben put in.

"That's my point," Griffin insisted. "The only difference between Luthor and the others is training."

"That's a big difference," Ben reminded him. "Especially since it's pretty obvious that we can't train him."

Griffin nodded sadly. Operation Doggie Rehab was a good plan, but it didn't consider the possibility that Luthor might be untrainable — except by Savannah, anyway

And she was out of the picture . . .

All at once, a surge of hope sizzled through his body like an electric current.

It wasn't necessarily true that Savannah was the only person who could train Luthor.

There was one other person who might be able to get through to the Doberman.

13

"What's a Trebezhov?"

Ben stood gasping in the front hall, struggling to catch his breath. One minute they'd been standing on the Drysdales' porch; the next he'd been running flat out, trying to keep up with Griffin, who was barreling at top speed through the streets of Cedarville. A brief stop at the Bing garage to drop off Luthor, then over to the Slovaks in an all-out sprint.

"Not *what*," Griffin explained, hyperventilating himself as he headed upstairs. "*Who*. Dmitri Trebezhov, the greatest dog trainer in history. Savannah told us about him, remember?"

Ben reached up to steady Ferret Face, who clung to his collar, reeling with motion sickness. "Wasn't he Electra's original handler?"

"Right," Griffin confirmed. "You see, the plan

was always fine. We just had the wrong people trying to execute it. If Dmitri Trebezhov can turn a
boring beagle into Super Mutt, just think what he
can do with Luthor."

Ben was skeptical. "Savannah said he disappeared off the face of the earth."

Griffin dismissed this with a shrug. "Everybody
has to be somewhere."

"Yeah, but the somewhere could be Antarctica,"
Ben argued. "What if he became a hermit, and he's
living on nuts and berries in a cave? When's the
last time anybody saw him? Three years ago? Face
it, Griffin, the guy could even be dead."

"I doubt it's anything like that," Griffin reasoned. "He probably quit the show circuit because
he got sick of vacuuming up dog hair. But now that
he's been on the sidelines a few years, he's dying
for an excuse to get back in the game. All we have
to do is find him."

There were no Trebezhovs in the phone book, and
a national directory search on the computer turned
up nothing. Google spat out more than two hundred
thousand hits on keywords *Dmitri Trebezhov*, but
these were mostly newspaper articles and blog post-
ings from his days as the brightest star in the dog
show cosmos. The boys browsed through hundreds

of accounts of the legendary handler's career — from age fifteen, when he knocked off a heavily favored borzoi with an underdog saluki in the hound group, to his glory days and the rise of Electra.

"Look at this," Ben said in awe. "During the blackout ten years ago, there were more than two thousand dogs trapped in the Manhattan Coliseum going nuts. Dmitri got up on stage with a bullhorn and calmed them all down. Savannah's right — he really is the world's greatest dog whisperer."

"We need an address." Griffin clicked on the link with the most recent post date, and another news story appeared on the monitor.

DOG WORLD'S "MAD RUSSIAN" HANGS UP HIS LEASH

NEW YORK — Dmitri Trebezhov, the most successful handler in the history of the professional dog show circuit, announced his retirement today, hours after his renowned Electra was named Best in Show at the annual Global Kennel Society competition. The bombastic Trebezhov called the event "a jumped-up flea circus," and his fellow handlers "backstabbing poop-scoopers in Armani suits." Then he removed his own clothing and left the Manhattan Coliseum in his underwear. By the time this reporter attempted to get in touch with him, Trebezhov's phone had been disconnected, and no one was answering the door at his residence. His website, www.dmitridogdude.usa, simply displays the message: GO AWAY.

The man seems to have vanished, and dog show enthusiasts are wondering why. . . .

There was a photograph of Trebezhov, a large man with a bowling ball of a head, shaved completely bald. The eyes fairly burned out of the picture.

"Boy," said Ben, "how'd you like to meet that guy in a dark alley?"

"Get used to it," Griffin advised. "He's our new trainer."

"Haven't you been paying attention?" Ben demanded. "There's been no sign of him for three years. If no one else can find him, what makes you think *we* can?"

"We have a secret weapon."

Melissa's room resembled the garbage Dumpster behind an electronics factory. The guts of the Spritz-o-matic lay strewn across the carpet from the edge of her single bed to the desk that held her four computers. The robot's shell leaned against her closet door, draped with yesterday's laundry. USB flash drives on a string hung from one of the spray nozzles.

Ben was blown away. "How do you get up and go to the bathroom in the middle of the night without breaking your neck over all this stuff?"

She agitated her head just enough to part her curtain of hair, revealing earnest eyes. "I know where everything is. This only seems like a mess. In my mind, it's totally orderly."

That was the amazing thing about Melissa. She lived in a state of chaos, but it wasn't chaotic to her. There was a place for everything, and everything was in its place.

"We need you to shift off the Spritz-o-matic for a little while," Griffin explained. "We're looking for a missing person. A dog trainer who might be able to help with Luthor. We don't know much about him, but his web page is www .dmitridogdude.usa."

Melissa was already at the keyboard. "This is a program I designed myself," she told them. "It can try twenty million password combinations a second. It should allow me to log into his site host as the webmaster. There," she added as the laptop sounded a beep. "I'm in. His password is 'LeaveMeAlone.' Are you sure this guy's a dog lover?"

"He likes his privacy," put in Griffin. "Have you got an address?"

"Here it is — whoops."

"What?" asked Ben. He and Ferret Face peered over Melissa's shoulder.

She swiveled the laptop so they could see the screen.

Mr. I. HateYou
1313 Deadend St.
Apt. 0
Pho, NY

"Griffin —" Ben looked a little nervous now. "This guy's nuts!"

"Are you allowed to do that?" Griffin asked Melissa. "Just use a fake name and address?"

Melissa continued to pound the keyboard. "There must be something real here. If he paid by credit card, there would have to be a billing address. Got it — uh-oh."

"Not again!" Ben exclaimed.

The Shaolin Palate Chinese Restaurant
2¹/₂ Packard Lane
Flushing, NY

"At least Flushing is a real place," Griffin offered.

Melissa opened a map program in a separate window. "The address checks out. It's in

Queens. In the city, about twenty miles west of here."

"We're going," Griffin decided.

"Are you crazy?" Ben squeaked. "Why are we going to a Chinese restaurant? The only thing we know about it is that whoever registered the website uses the name *I. HateYou*! What if he's violent?"

Griffin shrugged. "We'll have Luthor with us."

"Luthor will help him kill us!"

Griffin was patient. "Look, all this *I. HateYou* stuff, and fake addresses, and pretending to be a Chinese restaurant — it fits perfectly with a guy who's dropped out and is trying to disappear."

"All the more reason why he's not going to be glad to see us!" Ben insisted.

"Yeah, but we're bringing him the greatest Doberman of all time!"

"Dogs are what made him drop out in the first place!" cried Ben. "Be reasonable!"

"I *am* being reasonable," Griffin said grimly. "He's our only hope."

14

Luthor's mood had plummeted since the dog show. He was mopey and irritable, and getting him onto the leash was a major operation. The big Doberman had no intention of submitting to another "bath" at the truck wash. Nor did he relish the idea of spending more time with Griffin and Ben. He couldn't put his paw on it, but since they were the only ones who ever visited him, surely his unhappiness had to be their fault.

Today, though, the boys had come prepared. At the first sign of Luthor's growling, Griffin pulled a pink, flowered pillowcase from his back pocket and held it under the dog's nose.

Luthor froze, his cropped ears standing up even straighter. The scent was unmistakable, even though he hadn't been close to it for more than a week.

Savannah.

On her last trip to feed the Drysdale menagerie, Melissa had borrowed the pillowcase from Savannah's bed. To Luthor's sensitive canine nose, it was like standing right beside the girl he adored.

"Look at him!" Griffin intoned. "It's too bad there's no dog show today. He'd *own*!"

Ben was cautious. "Maybe he thinks this means she's coming back for him. What's he going to do when she doesn't show up?"

"We'll be in Flushing by then," Griffin said confidently. "With the best dog whisperer in the world. If Dmitri can't talk him down, nobody can."

The collar slipped easily around Luthor's neck, and they led him out of the garage. Bewitched by the scent of the pillowcase stuffed under Griffin's belt, he followed, meek as a lamb. He didn't even try to drag them in the direction of the Drysdale house, and showed no panic at all as they passed the truck wash on their way to the commuter station.

Once on the train, they settled into a deserted car. On their seat, a coffee spill had been soaked up with a copy of the morning paper. The tabloid was open to a story headlined:

DOGGONE PERFECT!

There, front and center, was a picture of Xerxes, the triumphant Yorkshire terrier, resplendent in his blue prize ribbon.

"I can't believe they gave Best in Show to that fluffed-up rat!" spat Ben in disgust. "I could put a rag mop on Ferret Face, and he'd look just as good."

Griffin peered over his shoulder. "Hey, they've got a list of all the winners. Do you see Luthor's name in there anywhere?"

Ben shook his head. "When you dream, you sure dream big! These are the winners, not the fleeing fugitives."

"They could have other categories," Griffin argued. "You know — Most Improved, Mr. Congeniality. Remember, they might have him down as Lex Luthor Savannah Spritz-o-matic."

"I think it's safe to say that Luthor avoided the winners' circle," Ben assured him. "But look — remember Emma, that girl who hates us? Her poodle, Jasmine, won Best in Group. According to this reporter, a lot of people had her figured to beat Xerxes for the top prize."

"Really? Is there a picture?" He snatched the paper from Ben's hand, planting a coffee stain on his lap.

Ben regarded him in surprise. "What's the big interest? She treated us like pond scum."

Griffin flushed and changed the subject. "Oh, look — a dog named Schroeder won for the Dobermans. I think he belongs to that idiot with the stick-out mustache who was bad-mouthing Luthor to the judge."

They gazed out the window as the train rattled along. The green of Long Island began to give way to the brick buildings and clogged roadways of New York's outer boroughs. They disembarked in Flushing and followed Melissa's map through the crowded streets. Although the sidewalks were jam-packed, space opened up in front of them as if by magic. Nobody wanted to tangle with the big dog.

Off the main drag, the streets were confusing, becoming a narrow and irregular grid. They found Packard Lane with some difficulty, and stood on the pavement, staring in dismay. There was number 2; there was number 4. On the opposite side was number 3. There was no $2^1/_2$ Packard Lane.

"Where's the restaurant?" Ben breathed. "Where's the Shaolin Palate?"

Griffin pointed wordlessly. At the edge of the building, where number 2 and number 4 met, five narrow, steep steps led down to an almost-hidden door that was covered by a faded sticker peeling off the glass window. It read:

THESE PREMISES
CONDEMNED BY ORDER
OF NYC BOARD OF HEALTH

In the marks left by what had once been brass numbers, they could make out a faint outline — $2^1/_2$. The only other window, almost opaque with dirt, was broken and partially boarded up.

Griffin cleaned off a small circle with his sleeve. "It used to be a restaurant," he confirmed. "I can see tables and chairs." He stepped back, his shoulders slumped with despair. "Why me?"

"Yeah," Ben agreed sarcastically. "Who would have thought that a classy place like this would ever be shut down by the Board of Health?"

"It's not the restaurant, it's the *plan*!" Griffin raved. "We're right back to square one! How are we going to find the guy now?"

It was as they were straggling back up the stairs, utterly defeated, that Ben tapped his friend on the shoulder. "Hey — if this place has been out of business for a long time, how come some guy is sweeping up in there?"

Griffin turned back. It was true. An indistinct figure, obscured by the dirty glass and the wood that sealed the broken window, was navigating a push broom across the floor of the derelict building.

He knocked on the window. "Hey, mister!"

The man didn't seem to hear him.

Griffin tried again, daring to knock harder this time. "Please — we have to ask you a question!"

A moment later, an immense shape appeared behind the CONDEMNED sticker. They heard the click of about seven locks, and the door opened to reveal a massive man with shoulder-length black hair, a bushy mustache, and a full beard.

"What question?" he growled.

"We're looking for someone — a famous dog handler named Dmitri Trebezhov," said Griffin.

"You may stop looking," said the big man. "The person you seek is dead."

Griffin was devastated. "How did he die?"

"It was a great tragedy. His hot-air balloon was shot down over a mine field. At least he did not suffer. Now, away with both of you and your dog and your weasel."

"He's a ferret!" Ben said to the slamming door.

For a long moment, they stood there, staring, but making no motion to leave.

It was Ben who finally broke the silence. "You know, I don't pretend to be the smartest person in the world, but this guy's full of it! Hot-air balloons and minefields! I'll bet he doesn't even know Dmitri Trebezhov!"

Griffin nodded glumly. "Maybe we're not the first people to show up looking for the guy. He's probably got a crazy story for everybody who knocks on that door. Let's blow this Popsicle stand."

They started up the stairs. Griffin tugged on Luthor's leash. "Come on, buddy. There's nothing for us here." Yet the dog was strangely reluctant to leave, and kept looking back as they ascended to street level. "Move it, Luthor. We've got a long ride home." Still the Doberman hesitated, and assumed a stubborn look that the boys recognized all too well.

"What's with him?" Ben complained. "He's acting like that's Disneyland back there."

"Tell me about it," groaned Griffin. "It's like trying to get him away from Savannah's house." He frowned at what he had just heard himself say. "In fact, it's *exactly* like trying to get him away from Savannah's house."

"That makes no sense at all," Ben scoffed. "Savannah's house was his home. This is an old restaurant, shut down by the health department."

"There might be one similarity," Griffin began slowly. "The Drysdales have a dog whisperer in residence. And if this place has one, too . . ."

15

Ben gawked. "You're not saying that Sasquatch is Dmitri Trebezhov! You saw the picture! It looks nothing like him! He was as bald as an egg!"

"Hair can be shaved," Griffin mused. "And it can grow back. Remember the eyes? Two black lasers? This guy has those eyes!"

Ben was beginning to come around. "He *does* seem like the kind of person who would register his website under *I. HateYou*."

Griffin clattered back down the stairs and rapped on the door. "Mr. Trebezhov, we know it's you. Open up."

"Go away."

"We can't," Ben pleaded. "We have a dog who needs you."

"Dmitri is no longer in the dog business."

Griffin seized on this. "But you were once! You were the greatest ever! And if you loved dogs then, you still love them now!"

The door opened a crack, and the hairy face appeared, laser eyes transfixing the boys. "Dmitri does not merely love dogs. They are my brothers and my sisters, and the sun that warms their fur also warms mine. It is because of this love that I reject any competition that imposes on dogs a standard of perfection no human could ever measure up to. Do you believe that, because dogs have no words, their souls are not crushed by the pressure we force on them? Enough! Your Doberman will thank me for sparing him the torment. Tails should never wag to impress a judge, but only from true happiness."

"But he'll *die*!" Griffin wailed.

The legendary handler took in Luthor's obvious health and vigor. "You are ridiculous. Why should he die?"

"You must have heard about what happened to Electra," Griffin began. "Well, Luthor is the dog who caused that whole accident."

The shaggy handler stiffened. "Is this true?"

"He didn't do it on purpose!" Ben jumped in.

"He just kind of — went nuts. It could happen to anybody!"

Griffin glared at him. "You're not helping!" he hissed.

But Dmitri addressed his comments to Luthor himself. "I thank you, my brother, and our sister Electra thanks you, too. Her life is once more her own. And although her tail is now crooked, she may wag it on her own terms."

"But that's only the start of it," Griffin insisted. He explained about the lawsuit, and how the Drysdales had been forced to give up Luthor to try to protect themselves financially. And he described the birth of Operation Doggie Rehab to turn Luthor into a show dog, and use his winnings to settle up with Electra's owners.

The burning eyes grew wide. "And you expect to do this in reality?"

Griffin nodded firmly. "That's the plan."

Dmitri Trebezhov threw back his head and brayed a laugh that rattled the shards of glass still in the window frame. "Commendable, my young friend. You are completely insane." And he slammed the door again.

"Well," Ben said resignedly, "I guess that's it. We did our best."

"We haven't even started!" said Griffin through clenched teeth.

Ben quailed. In all the years he had known Griffin, he had never seen such intensity on the face of The Man With The Plan. It was downright scary.

Griffin ripped Savannah's pillowcase out from under his belt, waved it in front of Luthor's nose, and then stuffed it through an iron grating down into the sewer below.

The whites of Luthor's eyes turned red like the hot coals of a fireplace. The angry bark that was torn from his throat drowned out the street noises from the city around them. There was nothing in the air but this dog and his all-consuming fury.

Ben did not hesitate. He climbed the nearest lamppost, and was four feet off the ground before daring to look down. What he saw almost stopped his heart. Griffin hadn't moved an inch, his jaw stuck out defiantly. Still roaring his anger, Luthor tensed, ready to spring at this human who had robbed him of his final connection to his beloved Savannah.

"Run!" Ben squeaked.

And then a third figure was on the scene. Dmitri Trebezhov interposed his six-foot-five-inch frame between Griffin and the enraged Doberman. Through his terror, Ben had to admit that he had never beheld anyone so calm, so peaceful, so serene. The dog whisperer raised a single pinkie finger, and held it steady until all Luthor's attention was focused on it.

Looking down from the pole, Ben could almost see the tension draining out of Luthor's muscular body. Dmitri lowered his hand, and the dog settled to the sidewalk as if manipulated by remote control. The big Russian dropped to his knees and gathered Luthor into his embrace, speaking soothingly: "Be calm, my brother. Life is hard, but we are strong, you and I."

Luthor whined submissively and nuzzled up to the handler. Ben dared to come down from the lamppost. He had only ever seen Luthor acting like this with Savannah. This man was not just a dog whisperer; he was a miracle worker!

Dmitri stroked the dog lovingly, murmuring endearments in English and Russian. All at once, the large man sat bolt upright, plucking something out of the ruff below Luthor's collar. "What is this?"

Ben squinted. "A thorn?"

Griffin looked closer. "It's metal. And pointy."

The handler's face was a thundercloud. "Dmitri will enlighten you. It is the tip of a dart. Note the small barbs near the point. Their purpose is to keep it lodged in the hide. And here" — he ruffled Luthor's short fur — "is the place where it broke the skin."

Griffin was mystified. "But why would anybody shoot Luthor?"

"Luthor was the target of the dart," Dmitri explained gravely, "but he was not the target of the attack. The dart was tipped with an irritating ointment designed to drive this poor fellow into a rampage. This is why he injured Electra at your mall. Someone made him do it."

"So you're saying that Luthor's *innocent*?" Ben asked, bug-eyed. "And the whole thing was an attack on Electra?"

The big man nodded. "You see now why Dmitri wants nothing more to do with the world of dog shows. The stakes are too high, the rewards too great, the competition too cutthroat, the handlers too ruthless. People will stop at nothing to better their position."

Griffin was irate. "This dog went to the pound! He could have been put down! It might still happen! Who would do such a horrible thing?"

"Anyone who stands to benefit from Electra's absence," Dmitri replied evenly. "And that means everybody. Electra was the number one dog in the world. With her out of competition, every other animal moves up one space."

"Maybe we should go to the cops," Ben suggested. "We can show them the dart and the puncture on Luthor's neck. That's proof that the accident wasn't his fault."

"It's only proof that we're trying to save our friend's dog." Griffin sighed. "For all the police know, we got the evidence at *Darts R Us*."

They lapsed into a melancholy silence, contemplating a bleak future. Of all the awful things that had happened, surely this was the worst. To have the evidence right in front of them, and to know that no one would ever believe it. Even Ferret Face wore a mournful expression as he nosed between the second and third buttons of Ben's shirt. They felt terrible for Luthor, for Savannah, and especially for themselves. The wasted hours, the futile planning, and the undeniable fact that neither would admit out loud — that they were coming to love this doomed dog they both still very much feared.

So wrapped up were they in their own unhappy

thoughts that they were totally unprepared for Dmitri's next words:

"I will do this thing."

"Huh?" Griffin managed.

"Dmitri will right this wrong by turning your Doberman into a great champion."

"That's *awesome* —" Griffin began.

"It is *not!*" the handler thundered. "I vowed never to return to that world. But return I must in order to save this magnificent animal."

Griffin turned to Ben. "See? I told you he was magnificent."

"He is not yet," the handler said smugly. "But when Dmitri is through with him, he will be."

16

Mr. Drysdale peered out the picture window of the lake house. His family was down on the thin strip of beach. The sun was shining, the water was sparkling, the day was perfect. Yet the black cloud that surrounded his daughter Savannah cast a gloom over an idyllic scene. Even from this distance, her melancholy was almost tangible. He could barely remember the last time he'd seen her smile, although he was sure he could name the date. June 26, the day before Electra's mall appearance that had changed everything.

And if Savannah's mood was a downer, the monkey, Cleopatra, was even worse. Clinical depression, the vet said. She had suggested a primate psychiatrist. The thought drove him mad. Two hundred dollars an hour to shrink the head of a capuchin monkey whose head couldn't really get very much smaller without disappearing. It was not a good investment for a man with a seven-million-dollar lawsuit hanging over his head.

His cell phone rang, and he picked up. "Rick Drysdale."

"Hi, Mr. Drysdale. It's Griffin Bing. Is Savannah there?"

"Sorry, she can't come to the phone. She's at the beach." For a moment, he toyed with the idea of running the cell out to his daughter. Maybe a familiar voice from home would be the cheering up she needed. Then again, home might be just another reminder of what she'd lost. He couldn't risk that.

"Could you ask her to call me at Ben Slovak's house?" Griffin requested. "We have good news. It turns out Luthor wasn't really responsible for what happened to Electra. Somebody shot him with a tiny dart to make him go nuts."

His daughter's friend had all Mr. Drysdale's attention now. "How could you possibly know something like that?"

"We found the dart and the puncture wound on Luthor's neck," Griffin explained.

For one brief shining instant, a seven-million-dollar weight began to lift from his bent shoulders.

Could this be true? Then he remembered who he was talking to — Griffin Bing, the king of cocka-mamie ideas. "Wait a minute!" Mr. Drysdale said suddenly. "Why do *you* have the dog? We left him at the pound!"

"I can't really go into all of it over the phone," Griffin said evasively. "But please give the mes-sage to Savannah, okay? There's a lot going on that she needs to know about."

"Certainly," said Mr. Drysdale, and hung up. There was only one thing certain about this call: Savannah was never going to hear of it. The Drysdale family was on the brink of disaster with this lawsuit. The last thing they needed was to involve The Man With The Plan.

For the second time that week, Griffin and Ben presented themselves at the door of $2^1/_2$ Packard Lane. Griffin inserted the small key in the lock behind the CONDEMNED sticker, and the two let them-selves into what was left of the Shaolin Palate.

Ben knew a moment's hesitation. "I hope Luthor's okay."

Griffin shrugged. "Why wouldn't he be? He's with the best dog trainer in history."

"That was three years ago," Ben retorted. "Today, the guy's Mr. I. HateYou. For all we know, the dog's chopped into fish bait, and we're next."

"Don't be such a baby," Griffin scoffed. But he had to admit there was something intimidating about walking through the wreckage of a long-abandoned restaurant with its broken and overturned furniture and peeling wallpaper. If Dmitri had been such a star, surely he'd made money. Why had he chosen to live in such a dump? Was it his weirdness, or was something else going on?

They found the staircase at the back and climbed up to the second floor. The sight that met their eyes at the top was such a contrast that both boys blinked. It was a large, open, loftlike space, filled with potted palms, exotic lamps, and Asian artwork. A serene Buddha, carved from dark wood, peered down at an apartment that was comfortable without being cluttered.

At the center of the room, Dmitri and Luthor sat on cushions, facing each other across a low table. A wooden tray of sushi sat between them. Griffin and Ben watched, transfixed, as Dmitri picked up a piece of tuna sashimi with a pair of carved chopsticks and held it out to the dog.

Luthor accepted the offering delicately, without ever touching the sticks with his mouth. Dmitri chose another piece and fed it to himself, equally delicately.

Ben was blown away. "They eat sushi at dog shows?"

Dmitri's burning eyes never left his pupil. "Millions of years of survival in the wild have taught my four-legged brothers and sisters to wolf down food, eating as quickly and as much as possible. If Luthor can control this impulse, he can control anything."

Griffin was impressed. "Normally when he eats you have to hold on to the wall to keep from getting sucked in!"

The Russian sighed tragically. "Just this last time," he vowed, "I will create one more canine robot for their perfect world, their Dog-topia." He turned moist eyes on the Doberman. "Forgive me, my brother."

Luthor burped, and then looked abashed.

"I don't think the wasabi agrees with him," Griffin offered.

Dmitri nodded. "We train the stomach as well." He lifted his pinkie finger. Instantly, Luthor was at his side. The handler placed the wooden sushi tray on the flat part of Luthor's large, wedge-shaped head. Taking graceful measured steps, the dog made his way to the kitchen with the tray perfectly balanced. He walked up to the trash can and depressed the pedal with his paw. The lid lifted. Slowly, and under tight control, Luthor inclined his head just enough so that the scraps on the tray slid into the garbage.

"Awesome!" Griffin breathed. "I can't believe you taught him all that in only three days!"

"I teach him nothing!" Dmitri said sharply. "All this is within him. I merely bring it out. Come with us, and you will see."

It was a small spit of land sticking out into Flushing Bay, the ground moist and soft. Citi Field, home of the Mets, was visible behind them. But otherwise, it seemed strangely removed from the rest of New York City.

Ben was mystified. "What kind of place is this to train a dog?"

The roar that followed sent both boys diving for cover. An American Airlines Airbus A320 screamed in directly over their heads, setting its landing wheels down on the runway of LaGuardia Airport, perhaps forty feet beyond them.

Ben held on to Ferret Face for dear life.

Griffin dug two hands into the turf as if he thought he could burrow under the grass and save himself. *"What was that?"*

"Unless I am mistaken," Dmitri told him mildly, "it was the 11:17 from Dallas, nine minutes late."

"Yeah, but why was it landing on top of us?" Ben whined.

In answer, the handler indicated Luthor, who had neither moved nor uttered a sound, but was totally focused on the upraised pinkie. "In a dog show, a champion must maintain absolute focus. If he can learn to ignore a landing airliner at close range, then he will not be distracted by a yappy dog on a nearby pedestal."

The Empire State Building was the tallest structure in New York, and the most famous skyscraper anywhere in the world. Griffin stood at the base of the stairwell, peering up at flights of steps that seemed to extend all the way to infinity.

Dmitri addressed his star pupil, pinkie raised. "Brother, you may be tempted to turn around before you reach the top. If you cheat, Dmitri will know."

Ben was horrified. "The *top* top? He's not going to win the dog show if he has a heart attack on the stairs!"

"A champion," Dmitri said imperiously, "knows no fatigue. And his heart is forged from iron."

They watched as Luthor jumped to his task, muscles rippling as he powered his way up. A moment later he was out of sight. A few minutes after that, they could no longer hear the clicking of his nails on the concrete steps.

The silence unnerved Griffin. "It's a long way up. What if he gets lost?"

Dmitri held out his pinkie. "He would return to *this* from beyond the grave."

They waited, five minutes, then ten.

"Maybe we should go up and get him," suggested Ben worriedly.

Dmitri glared at him. "I do not seek the sun at midnight, because I know it will return at dawn. Go if you wish. Your leg cramps do not concern Dmitri."

Around the fifteen-minute mark, the toenail clicking returned. Luthor burst out of the stairwell, and came to sit quietly in front of the pinkie.

"Excellent," approved Dmitri. "Tomorrow — the Chrysler Building."

Next stop was Wall Street and the New York Stock Exchange. An old dog show contact of Dmitri's got them visitors' badges, and they were admitted to the floor. Luthor, of course, had no badge, but no one was willing to question the big dog's right to go wherever he wanted.

If there was any order to this place, Griffin and Ben were unable to detect it. It was pure chaos. People ran in all directions through a blizzard of airborne paper, everyone outshouting everyone else. The voices melded into one constant din that reminded them of the LaGuardia runway.

Griffin and Ben hung back, sweating in their borrowed, oversized blazers. No matter how strong the air conditioning was, it simply couldn't keep up with the action and body heat of the place. But Luthor and Dmitri were just a blur. They circled the exchange floor at high speed, Luthor at the end of a short leash. Dmitri's long strides were taxed to the limit to keep pace. All around them — in front of them, behind them, and on either side — frantic people dashed to and fro, shouting instructions, waving transaction slips, buying and selling billions of dollars in stocks.

It should have been a demolition derby, with traders, agents, and pages tripping over dog and leash, and bouncing off of the big Russian. There should have been bumps, bruises, and many dog bites. Instead, Luthor and Dmitri passed through the roiling mob like ghosts, touching no one, yet never slowing down or altering course.

"You know" — Ben had to shout just to be heard — "that guy is a few sandwiches short of a picnic, but I'm starting to believe he knows his stuff."

Griffin had a completely different take on the matter. Operation Doggie Rehab, which had been dead in the water a few short days ago, was beginning to look as if it might actually work.

The plan was back.

Dmitri Trebezhov in a bathing suit was an astounding sight. His skin was milk-white, like he had never been in the sun in his life. Tattooed on this pristine canvas was the portrait of every dog he had ever handled. Skinny legs, also startlingly white, supported an enormous, muscular frame, and his long, dark hair and beard stood out straight from his face, held aloft by a stiff sea breeze.

Hot, sunny weather had brought a large, happy crowd to Rockaway Beach that afternoon. A multitude of towels and blankets made the sand resemble a patchwork quilt. Frisbees and footballs flew in all directions, and a spirited volleyball game, twenty players a side, filled the air with shouts and good-natured arguments. Ice cream and drink vendors circulated among the bathers, hawking their wares. Everything was active, in motion. Except Luthor.

The Doberman stood at the water's edge, absolutely motionless, and perfectly stacked. Swimmers and boogie boarders frolicked all around him. A dropped Popsicle lay on the sand three inches in front of his nose. His focus remained absolute.

The wave seemed to come out of nowhere, a wall of water that rose suddenly from the ocean. It exploded over Luthor, swamping him completely. For a moment, he was gone, lost in the foam. When the breaker receded, there was the big Doberman, soaked, half-buried in seaweed — still perfectly stacked as if nothing had ever happened.

Griffin stared, unable to believe his own eyes. "But he *hates* water! When we put him through the truck wash, he got totally bent out of shape about it!"

Dmitri glared at him "Perhaps that is because he is not a truck. He is a dog. And he will be a virtuoso, in spite of your efforts to traumatize him."

"A virtuoso?" Ben repeated. "Are you saying what I think you're saying?

Dmitri nodded. "He is ready."

17

"I think we should write a letter to the Parks Department," announced Mrs. Slovak as the car merged onto the Long Island Expressway. "They're not cleaning the pool properly. The last time I did the boys' laundry, I could have sworn there was sand in their bathing suits."

In the backseat, Griffin and Ben exchanged agonized glances.

"Maybe it's the chlorine crystallizing," Ben suggested hopefully.

"I don't think it works that way," mused his father at the wheel.

It was the Slovaks' wedding anniversary, and the family and their semipermanent houseguest were headed into New York City to the Italian restaurant where Ben's parents had gone for their first date.

"It's really nice of you to let me crash your celebration," said Griffin, anxious to change the subject.

"We weren't going to leave you at home to eat bread and water." Ben's father laughed.

His wife laughed, too, but not as heartily.

Trattoria Cinque Fratelli was exactly as the Slovaks remembered it. And — what luck! — they were able to get the same table they'd occupied as a courting couple. They sat down and began to peruse the menu in a leisurely manner.

"What do you hear from your parents, Griffin?" Mr. Slovak asked.

"I just Skyped them last night," Griffin replied. "Their trip's okay, but you know Dad. He's only happy when he's in his workshop, tinkering." He had a giddy vision of the state of that workshop right now. In the heat of Operation Doggie Rehab, there had been no time to tidy up after Luthor's rampage. The only tinkering going on was in Melissa's room, where the Spritz-o-matic was dismantled to its wires and components.

"Unbelievable!" Mrs. Slovak's expression radiated shock and anger. She pointed. "That man — his dinner companion is a *dog*!"

They followed her pointing finger. Ben kicked

Griffin under the table, but Griffin had already made the identification. There in a corner booth sat none other than Dmitri Trebezhov. And his companion was indeed a dog.

Luthor.

The Doberman sat upright on the banquette, his proud head poised over an enormous plate of pasta. He was delicately eating linguine, a single strand at a time, sucking it up with total discipline and concentration.

Mr. Slovak was amazed. "It certainly has excellent table manners."

"Table manners? It's a *dog*! It's not even allowed to enter a restaurant, much less to be a customer!"

Ben tried to calm her down. "Come on, Mom. Live and let live."

She would not be soothed. "I get out on the town once in a blue moon! I don't ask to rub elbows with millionaires and celebrities. But I don't think it's too much to expect that my fellow diners should be human!"

She made such a fuss that the maître d' tiptoed over. "Is there a problem, signora?"

"I'd call it a problem! Why is there a dog over there slurping noodles?"

"He's not slurping," Ben pointed out. "He's actually pretty quiet."

"Do you not recognize the gentleman?" asked the maître d'. "That is Dmitri Trebezhov, the greatest dog handler in the world."

"That doesn't change the fact that it's unsanitary to allow an animal into a restaurant!" Mrs. Slovak insisted.

The maître d's eyes traveled to Ben's shirt and Ferret Face, who was leaning out, nibbling sesame seeds off a breadstick.

Mr. Slovak spoke up swiftly. "He's a medical ferret. We have a doctor's letter. Would you like to see it?"

"That will not be necessary," the maître d' said graciously. "Enjoy your dinner." And he walked away.

"If I didn't know better," Mr. Slovak commented, "I'd swear that dog was Savannah Drysdale's Doberman. But this animal's far too well behaved."

Mrs. Slovak addressed the boys, who were both bright red and stiff-lipped. "Now look — I've spoiled your evening. I promise I'll drop the subject."

In reality, the source of their discomfort was the fear that Dmitri would see them and wish them a hearty hello. Then they would be required to explain the unexplainable.

Griffin didn't taste a bite of his dinner. It all went straight down, and lay like lead in his stomach. His one hope was that eating linguini one strand at a time was a slow process, and that the Slovak party might be finished and gone before Dmitri and Luthor would walk right past their table on the way out.

No such luck. A strangled sound escaped Ben as Dmitri and his pupil rose to leave. Man and dog grew closer as Griffin's personal doomsday clock counted down to zero. Dmitri cleared his throat to speak.

Oh, don't! Oh, please! Oh, no!

"Excuse us," the big Russian said politely, sidling around their table, Luthor in tow. Seconds later, they were on the street. The door of the restaurant closed behind them.

"I — I have to go to the bathroom!" Griffin sprinted for the restroom sign, but doubled back around the bar and slipped out through a service exit, finding himself in a narrow alley. He raced to the street just as Dmitri was loading Luthor into a taxi.

"Hey — wait!" He caught up to them, panting.

"Thanks for not giving us away in front of Ben's parents!"

"Dmitri is not stupid. If Luthor was the family dog, I would be dealing with the family, not with two children."

"Ben's mom almost had a fit!" Griffin exclaimed. "Do you always take dogs to restaurants?"

"Pasta before a show. That is the rule."

"But the Global Kennel Society show isn't for two more weeks," Griffin pointed out.

Dmitri shook his head. "No, he cannot enter that one."

"What?" All the color drained from Griffin's face. "Then what are we doing this for? The whole point of the plan was to win at Global!"

"Calm yourself," Dmitri advised. "No dog may enter Global without a Best of Breed victory at another competition."

Griffin was distraught. "So what can we do?"

"The Mid-Atlantic Kennel Society is holding its summer show tomorrow in Metuchen, New Jersey. My brother's performance there will qualify him for Global."

Griffin's head was spinning. He didn't want to fight with Dmitri, but this was bizarre. Luthor was going into competition. And they would have had no way of knowing about it if they hadn't, by sheer random chance, run into the pair carbo-loading at one out of tens of thousands of restaurants in New York City!

"When were you planning to tell us about this?" Griffin demanded. "He's our dog — until it's okay for him to go back to our friend Savannah!"

Dmitri shrugged. "In that case, would you care to join us?"

"Ben and I would be delighted!"

18

Emma Hightower fluffed the white pouf around Jasmine's crown. "There, beautiful girl," she cooed. "Some poodles shed in the summer, but not you."

Her mother joined her in the benching area, hefting a carton filled with sprays, brushes, picks, and canine hair products. "The parking lot's already a mess," she commented, shedding her silver raincoat and running a hand through her bright red hair.

"Mid-Atlantic's always the last show before Global," Emma reminded her. "Everyone uses it as a rehearsal for the big time."

Mrs. Hightower plugged a blow-dryer into a large power strip that had been set up for use by the contestants. "Let's give her a final once-over."

"She doesn't need it," said Emma. "She's perfect."

"You might want to rethink that." Mrs. Hightower turned a jaundiced eye toward the center aisle, where Mrs. Devlin was making an entrance with her little Xerxes in her arms. The Yorkshire terrier's win on Long Island had cemented his position as the clear favorite at Global.

Emma made a face. "I looked into that judge's eyes, and I'm positive hc liked Jazzy as much as Xerxes. He just picked the Yorkie because it was his turn after playing second fiddle to Electra for so long." Her eyes fell on a figure coming in the gate, and she uttered a snort of disgust. "Well, I never thought *he'd* have the nerve to show his face at another dog show!"

Griffin Bing smiled and waved, working his way through the crowd toward her. His skinny sidckick — Ben? — was right behind him.

She lowered her head and busied herself fluffing the poodle's tail.

"I'm going to go and say hello to Mercedes Devlin," her mother announced.

"Don't leave me here alone with —" Emma

hissed. But it was too late. Mrs. Hightower was already gone, and the boys were upon her.

"Hi, Emma," Griffin said. "Hi, Jasmine. How's it going?"

"Great. You probably heard that Jazzy won her group on Long Island. Oh, wait — you weren't there for the end. You were chasing your dog all over town."

Griffin flushed.

Ben bristled. "He's way better than that now. We hired a new handler." He looked over his shoulder. "Here he comes."

Emma had been noticing a buzz of excitement at the entrance to the benching area. At that moment she spotted the bearded trainer at the other end of the leash around Luthor's collar. "Who's that, the world's tallest hippie?"

A short, slight reporter was at the head of the throng, jogging backward to keep pace with Dmitri's long-legged strides. "I'm with the *Canine Chronicle*, Mr. Trebezhov," she puffed. "Can I ask you a few questions?"

"Trebezhov?" Emma's jaw dropped. "Your new handler is *Dmitri Trebezhov*? But — that looks nothing like him!"

"He grew a lot of hair in his time away from the dog show circuit," Ben supplied.

Emma was bug-eyed. "How did you get him? No one's seen him in years! He left and swore he'd never come back!"

"He hadn't met Luthor yet," Griffin said smugly.

She was unconvinced. "Are you rich? Your dad paid him a ton of money to come out of retirement, right?"

"No!"

"What kind of car do you have?" she pushed.

By that time, the crowd around Dmitri reached them, and there was too much chaos for conversation.

When Mrs. Devlin recognized the legendary handler, she was so shocked that she dropped Xerxes. The Yorkie hit the ground like a furry ball, bounced, and began scrambling up her leg.

"I'm speaking with Dmitri Trebezhov, who has returned from self-imposed exile to bring an unknown dog to the Mid-Atlantic show." The reporter struggled to keep her voice steady as she stutter-stepped along. "Mr. Trebezhov, what's the best part of being back?"

"Knowing I can leave again," the big Russian

replied, deadpan. "Dmitri still despises the dog show."

The reporter stared at him but came back gamely. "Tell us about the dog. We're all curious about Lex Luthor Savannah Spritz-o-matic."

"He has four legs and a tail," Dmitri offered blandly. "He does not play the harpsichord. He has never been to Pakistan."

Emma had been moving closer to Griffin and Ben in the hope of being introduced to their famous handler. This brought Jasmine and Luthor face-to-face. They seemed to be pleased to meet again, and touched noses in a familiar and affectionate way. When Luthor showed signs of becoming a little love-struck, the pinkie finger came up to call him back to his duty.

The schedule was nearly identical to the Long Island show, but the day could not have been more different. Dmitri was in control, which took some of the pressure off of Griffin and Ben. For his part, Dmitri didn't seem to feel any pressure at all. While other owners and handlers primped and brushed their dogs, he lay in the dirt and grass of the benching area, reading to Luthor from an ancient copy of *Lassie Come-Home*. The Doberman was paying rapt attention, peering over his trainer's shoulder as if following along.

At last, the announcement came. Dobermans — open class. Dmitri carefully marked his place by folding the corner of the page, and led his pupil to ring two. Although the other handlers were dressed conservatively in black and muted shades, Dmitri resembled a commune leader at the height of the 1960s, resplendent in DayGlo orange. Yes, the strategy was to fade into the background and highlight the dog — unless the handler happened to be the immortal Dmitri Trcbezhov.

Griffin felt the familiar buzz of nervous electricity that always came when a plan reached a make-or-break moment. If Luthor could not pass this first test, Operation Doggie Rehab would crash and burn. Everything was hanging on the next few minutes.

Ben nudged Griffin. "Uh-oh, look who's here. Mr. Mustache."

There, talking to the judge a mile a minute, was the man with the long waxed mustache. Schroeder, his Doberman, was at his side. The judge, an older woman, was taking it all in, nodding.

She approached Dmitri. "Mr. Trebezhov, it's an honor to meet you. There seems to be some concern that the size of your dog might indicate a mixed breed."

Dmitri bristled. "Look at him. He is an exact copy of the others. There is not a single feature that differs from them."

"Except his *size*," she persisted, "which might indicate Great Dane or even mastiff. According to the breed standard —"

"When a dog is too large, this will show itself in other ways. His proportions will be off, also his gait. Perhaps his hocks will meet the ground at an incorrect angle. He will not stack properly. But if he is perfect in every way, it is the breed standard that is lacking — not the dog."

The wisdom of this — and the fact that it had come from Dmitri himself — seemed to satisfy the judge. She nodded briskly and called the handlers into the ring.

"Think Luthor can do it?" Ben whispered anxiously.

Griffin shrugged. "I don't know. It's one thing to run up the Empire State Building, but I don't see any skyscrapers around. The only way to win here is with dog show stuff. And I didn't see Luthor practice much of that."

Yet as the dogs began to circle the ring, Griffin had a vision of the Doberman navigating the mob scene on the floor of the stock exchange. When they were called upon to stack, he remembered Luthor at the beach, not flinching even when an ice-cold wave washed over him. And when the judge began the physical examination that had knocked Luthor out of the last show, Griffin pictured the dog at the airport, unperturbed even as large jets roared in overhead.

Luthor aced everything. But, to Griffin's untrained eye, so did the others. It was all in the judge's hands now. Would the accusations from Mr. Mustache manage to plant just enough suspicion in the judge's mind to keep Luthor out of the winner's circle?

The answer came immediately, but Griffin wasn't quite sure what to make of it.

"Number fourteen, number three, number eleven, number five." There was polite applause.

Ben frowned. "What's that supposed to mean?"

Griffin caught sight of the number on Dmitri's armband: 14.

"We won," he whispered. Relief flooded over him, and he struggled to keep his emotions under control. All this meant was that Luthor would move on to compete for Best of Breed. Without a victory at that level, he would not qualify for Global.

"Well, what do you know," Ben blurted. "Luthor's the real deal!"

"And Dmitri," Griffin added.

Dmitri was unimpressed by the victory. "This was kindergarten. My brother should win this with one paw tied behind his back."

Two chapters of *Lassie Come-Home* later, the Doberman was back in action, this time vying for Best of Breed. Decisions had come quickly in the open class, but *this* judge was taking forever. His physical inspection was so slow and thorough that Griffin was positive Luthor was going to turn and bite the official's head off. Only the mystical power of Dmitri's pinkie kept his pupil still and focused.

"Come on, dude, don't make a science out of it," Ben murmured under his breath, exhorting the judge. "Grab one pooch's butt, you've grabbed them all."

Ferret Face, sensing the tension, whined softly.

The waiting did not end there. The dogs circled the ring endlessly as the deliberate man marched around, examining them from several different angles.

For Griffin, it was pure torture. This was the competition that *really* counted. A Best of Breed win would catapult Luthor to Global. Anything less — even second place — would send him home. That meant the pound, and a terrible fate.

Hurry up!

19

The judge stepped back. He had reached his decision. His arm came up, his pointer finger panning the Dobermans.

Griffin shut his eyes.

The finger stopped, trained on Luthor. "Number fourteen —"

Other numbers followed, but Griffin didn't hear any of them. He was already leaping over the fence, punching the air, and cheering at the top of his lungs. Ben was right behind, and if his celebration was a little more restrained, it was only for the sake of Ferret Face, who didn't like noise.

"Luthor — you did it, man!" Griffin was about to throw his arms around the newly crowned Best of Breed, when Dmitri stepped in front of him.

"You embarrass yourself," he said sternly. "And you embarrass my brother."

But Luthor didn't look embarrassed. He looked vaguely pleased with himself. He knew he'd won something.

"So what happens now?" asked Ben. "Maybe we should pull him out — you know, quit while we're ahead."

"That's not a bad idea," Griffin agreed. "Like resting your starters when you've got a big lead. We've already got what we came for. Winning another round doesn't do any good. It could only hurt us if Luthor goes berserk and gets banned from competition."

"You do not interrupt da Vinci while he is painting the *Mona Lisa*," Dmitri proclaimed. "Nor do you replace a pitcher after eight innings of a perfect game. And you do not stand between a dog and his destiny."

"But this *isn't* his destiny," Griffin argued. "The Global show is. Shouldn't we save him for that?"

"Never ration greatness," the handler lectured. "It is bigger than you. It is even bigger than Dmitri."

Back in the benching area, Emma was packing away her poodle's latest Best of Breed ribbon in a velvet box containing many others. Spying the boys, she said, "You guys are still here? I thought you'd be chasing your dog down the Garden State Parkway by now."

"That shows what you know," Ben retorted. "Luthor just won Best of Breed, so we'll be hanging around for a while. We might be hanging around longer than you."

Griffin shot Ben a dirty look and beamed at Emma. "Congratulations on Jasmine's win. I guess we'll be seeing you at Global."

She cleared her throat in annoyance. "If you're going to be Global, we have to set some ground rules. Jazzy and I have worked too hard to have a big galoot like Luthor come along and get her thinking about romance instead of ribbons."

"We don't want Luthor getting distracted, either," Griffin agreed. "Let's talk about it. It's lunch break anyway. Care for a sandwich?"

Ben stared openmouthed.

"Oh — no, thanks," Emma said quickly. "I should eat with my mom." She looked around hopefully. Mrs. Hightower was nowhere to be seen.

Griffin held out a roll piled high with corned beef. "We've got plenty."

She made a face. "I'm a vegetarian."

While Emma dug through piles of hair products

for the cooler that contained her lunch, Ben snatched the sandwich out of Griffin's hands.

" 'We've got plenty!' " he mimicked savagely. "That was *my* food you gave away!"

"But I didn't."

"You *tried* to! If your girlfriend ate meat, I'd be begging puppy chow from the cocker spaniels!"

"She's not my girlfriend!" Griffin hissed.

"You want her to be. Why else would you be kissing up to her when she treats you like garbage? What's the deal with that, Griffin? How does *she* fit into Operation Doggie Rehab?"

"It can't hurt to get along with the other owners and handlers —"

Ben cut him off. "There are no bonus points for making friends in the dog show! I've known you all my life. This is the first time I've ever seen The Man With The Plan take his eyes off the ball —"

Emma put an end to their argument when she sat down beside them on the grass, a large Tupperware of salad balanced on her lap. "Where are Luthor and Mr. Trebezhov?"

Griffin took a bite of his own sandwich. "They're at some trattoria in town. Dmitri's got a thing about dog shows and pasta. Did you figure out where your mom is?"

"I saw her on the other side of the campus with Mercedes Devlin. She does nothing but bad-mouth that woman, but she never passes up a chance to hang out with her." Emma grinned. "Probably looking for an opening to kick Xerxes down a storm drain."

"Is Xerxes really that good?" Griffin asked.

She shrugged. "He is. But my Jazzy is better. The problem is once the judges see a dog as number one, it's almost impossible to break into that spot. Xerxes spent years in Electra's shadow. I'm just worried that the same thing is going to happen to Jazzy — always second place behind Xerxes." The poodle came up beside her, nuzzling her neck and chin. "Don't listen to me, girl. Today will be our day. I can feel it!"

"I can feel it, too," added Griffin. Now that Luthor had qualified for Global, he could afford to be generous.

She smiled timidly. "What's it like to work with Dmitri Trebezhov? He's a legend, but he has a reputation for being kind of odd."

"He's a total wack job," Griffin said honestly. "And definitely the president of his own fan club. But when it comes to dogs, he rocks. You wouldn't believe the kind of training he does. It's pretty off the chain."

Ben finished his sandwich and stood up. "I hope nobody minds if I go to the bathroom," he announced, miffed at being completely ignored. When Griffin didn't even turn in his direction, he added, "By the way, Dmitri called. Luthor was struck by a falling satellite. He's got a solar panel sticking out of one ear, and that's not in the breed standard."

"Yeah, great," Griffin said absently. He had Emma's attention. Nothing else seemed as important as that.

Soon the bell rang to end the lunch break and call the dogs and handlers to the next event — the group competition.

As the top Doberman, Lex Luthor Savannah Spritz-o-matic was in the "working" group, which included guard dogs, sled dogs, hunting and fishing companions, and rescue dogs. They made a motley assortment as they took their places beside pedestals marked with their breeds. There was everything from the short-haired, all-business Rottweiler to the fuzzy, web-footed Newfoundland. There was a strange creature called a komondor that resembled a lamb with dreadlocks. The Great Dane and Neapolitan mastiff dwarfed even Luthor.

The handler of the giant schnauzer looked more like a bank president, perfectly groomed with a Hollywood hairdo and a four-thousand-dollar suit. He took in Dmitri's bright orange poncho. "I see your sense of style hasn't changed."

"Only one dog, Nigel?" Dmitri returned. "You are usually not without three or four."

"Try seven," Nigel informed him. "I have assistants handling the others. Business is good."

"I am delighted that you have gained so much from Dmitri's retirement," the big Russian said graciously.

The perfectly coiffed man flushed. "We're equals here. Two handlers at group."

Dmitri nodded. "With one exception. I am Dmitri. And you are not."

Griffin and Ben leaned over the gate. "Who's that guy? He doesn't like you very much."

Dmitri dismissed the question. "He is nobody. If he has had any success, it is because he handles so many dogs that one of them is bound to win by sheer random chance."

If the judging had been confusing in the early rounds, here at group it was a total mystery.

"I sort of understand how you pick the best Doberman," Ben wondered aloud. "But how do you compare Luthor to a sled dog or that sheep thing? It's like trying to decide what's better — a bowling ball or toilet paper."

Griffin was reading the show brochure. "According to this, you pick the dog who matches his own breed standard better than the other dogs match theirs. Anyway, it doesn't matter who wins this. We've already qualified for Global."

Yet as soon as Dmitri led Luthor out into the ring, they just knew. Every step, every motion of his head, his gait, his carriage, the movement of his muscles underneath his shiny coat — all perfection. And when the judge announced that the winner was the Doberman, they were happy, but unsurprised. Dmitri had used the word *destiny*. That seemed to be exactly what was unfolding here.

There was only one more competition scheduled that day. More than nine hundred dogs had entered the Mid-Atlantic show. Now only seven remained. The group winners gathered in the center ring. It was time to determine which animal would take home the top prize.

Best in Show.

20

It had all come down to this supercharged moment.

Luthor represented the working group. From the terriers, there was an Airedale with a coat as lustrous as gold leaf; from the sporting group, a fiery red Irish setter; from herding, a Welsh corgi whose short stature did nothing to diminish a regal bearing; from the hounds, a sleek, aero-dynamically perfect greyhound handled by none other than Dmitri's well-dressed rival, Nigel Diamond; from non-sporting, Jasmine, white and immaculate, Emma at her side; and from the toy group, Xerxes, now the number-one dog in the world. It was the cream of the canine crop. The fact that Luthor had gone from the Cedarville pound to here in a matter of weeks would have been ridiculous if it hadn't been so remarkable.

To Griffin, it was the plan, working out in all its glory.

There was a tense delay, as everyone waited for the judge to arrive. It was dog show tradition that the person who decided Best in Show came in totally cold. At last she was there, shorter than the Great Dane, squatter than the dachshund, with an expression that would not have been out of place on the face of the bloodhound.

It started again: stacking, gaiting, physical examination. It was the same old same old, yet the moment seemed bigger somehow. All eyes were riveted on the competitors. The silence was total, the crowd holding its collective breath. Even Ferret Face ventured far enough out of Ben's shirt to watch the drama unfold.

"Any idea who's winning?" Ben whispered.

Griffin shrugged. The judge seemed to be paying the most attention to Xerxes and Jasmine, her sharp eyes alternating between the Yorkie and the poodle. Emma's words came back to him: *Today will be our day.* For her sake, he hoped so.

And then the verdict came down. The woman spun on her heel in an about-face and pointed at Luthor. "The Doberman."

Griffin swayed dangerously, coming closer to

fainting than he'd ever come before. The buzz of surprise nearly drowned out the applause, and a chorus of *yes, buts*:

"Yes, but he's a total unknown . . ."

"Yes, but his handler is Trebezhov . . ."

"Yes, but he's huge for his breed . . ."

"Yes, but he's in perfect proportion . . ."

Everyone seemed to have an opinion, but only one mattered — the judge's. Luthor, the world's most oversized underdog, had won Best in Show.

It took Ben to haul Griffin over the fence so they could rush the ring. The Doberman seemed pleased but a little bewildered by all the attention.

"Dmitri — you did it!" Ben cheered.

The big Russian looked as if he had lost his only friend. "Dmitri has turned this noble animal into a preening robot. I should be shot."

Cameras flashed as Luthor was draped with an enormous blue ribbon. Reporters shouted questions, but the winning handler wouldn't answer any of them.

"Go away," he told them. "Dmitri hates himself. Don't make me hate you, too."

The press quoted him word for word. The inimitable Dmitri Trebezhov was back.

The benching area had mostly cleared out by the time the triumphant Team Spritz-o-matic returned to collect their belongings.

Emma was packing up cartons of hairspray and sheen.

"Great show, Emma!" Griffin congratulated. "I really thought Jasmine was going to win it all today."

"You *jerk*!" she hissed.

Griffin was taken aback.

Her eyes fairly shot sparks. "Jazzy and I have worked and slaved for *years* to get where we are today! You wouldn't know a dog from a wildebeest, and you drop out of the sky with that big, stupid Doberman and hire the best trainer in history so nobody else has a chance! You're nothing but a selfish, clueless, rich doofus!" And she hefted her boxes and stormed off.

"He's not rich!" Ben called after her.

Griffin held his head. "First she couldn't stand me because Luthor was so hopeless. And now that he's better, she can't stand me even worse!"

Dmitri clucked sympathetically. "Excellence is a terrible burden. Oh, how Dmitri has suffered."

It wasn't until they headed for the parking lot

that the full weight of Griffin's exhaustion pressed down on him.

"Can you believe it's been only twelve hours since we got on the train for Dmitri's place this morning?" he said to Ben.

Ben nodded wearily. "It feels like months. I mean, Luthor started the day as a nobody; now he's a champion."

"The plan seemed like a one-in-a-million shot," Griffin added. "Now it's totally back on track. You have to figure Luthor is one of the favorites to win it all at Global."

"And this morning you were toe jam to Emma. Now you're still toe jam — but for a totally different reason." Ben stopped in front of Dmitri's 1971 Volkswagen Bus and plucked a piece of paper from under the windshield wiper. "Bummer. We got a ticket."

Dmitri and the boys examined the crumpled page. The message was written in mismatched letters cut from newspaper headlines and taped in place.

tHE DobERmAn'S LifE iS in gRAVe DanGEr
dRoP OuT WhILe yOu stILL caN
nO dOgGoNe jOkE

166

Ben's eyes scoured the deserted parking lot. "Who put this here?"

"I guess somebody who doesn't want to face Luthor at Global," Griffin reasoned.

The handler nodded slowly. "If you eliminate Luthor, you eliminate Dmitri."

Ben was uneasy. "I don't like this, Griffin. This guy sounds dangerous to me."

"Why?" Griffin shot back. "Because he has scissors and Scotch tape? The whole thing is probably a joke."

"It says no joke!"

"No *doggone* joke," Griffin amended. "Don't you know kennel humor when you hear it?"

"It is no joke," Dmitri concluded in a somber tone. "You do not threaten the life of a dog unless you are deadly serious. The stakes, the money, the fame — it drives people to madness. It is not for me anymore. Despite my magnificence, Dmitri is a simple man."

"Operation Doggie Rehab was supposed to be about helping Luthor," Ben argued. "How does it help him to risk getting him killed?"

"How can we quit now, when the plan is finally coming together?" Griffin returned.

"Enough!" Dmitri held up his pinkie. Luthor

snapped to attention, and Griffin and Ben fell silent. The boys had not understood the power of the simple gesture until that very moment. "Dmitri did not ask to return to the dog show. But now that I am back, there will be no quitting."

"But the author of the note could be a deranged psycho!" Ben protested.

"Possibly," the big Russian agreed. "But Luthor does not know the meaning of threats. And Dmitri does not know the meaning of fear."

21

MID-ATLANTIC CHAMP LINKED TO TOP DOG'S ACCIDENT

METUCHUN, NJ — The dog world is buzzing about Lex Luthor Savannah Spritz-o-matic, an oversized Doberman who took top honors at the prestigious Mid-Atlantic Kennel Society show this past weekend. The previously unknown dog was presented by none other than Dmitri Trebezhov, the fabled handler — now a virtual hermit — who suddenly returned to competition just for this animal.

That story would be newsworthy enough, but the *Times* has learned that Luthor, the newly minted Best in Show, is the unruly animal responsible for the mall accident that sidelined the previous number-one dog, Electra Mourning Becomes Eugene. The beagle — originally trained by Trebezhov himself — had been on the verge of an unprecedented fourth-straight Global Kennel Society victory. Her owners declined to comment due to a pending lawsuit.

Dog lovers have much to think about in this new champion, who poses more questions than he answers: How could such a newbie come out of nowhere, and attract the greatest trainer in the history of the sport? How could a dog that goes berserk at a mall be capable of the kind of poise and discipline required of a Best in Show? And most important of all, can he win the big one — the 136th annual Global Kennel Society show in New York City next week?

If Lex Luthor Savannah Spritz-o-matic can accomplish that, all the other questions will blow away like the dust of a well-used dog run. . . .

"I don't like it." Ben crumpled up the article and tossed it in a trash bin. "This reporter is practically saying that Dmitri trained his new dog to knock out his old dog so he could get back in the spotlight."

The two were headed over to Griffin's house to take in the Bings' mail.

Griffin had a different worry. "Good thing my parents are in Prague. The last thing we need is my dad seeing that article."

"What are you talking about? It doesn't mention us."

"It doesn't have to," Griffin replied grimly. "It says *Spritz-o-matic*. A new invention is supposed to be a secret. You don't name a championship dog after it. I should have told that lady his name was Fred."

"You can't plan for everything," Ben offered comfortingly.

It earned him a sharp look from Griffin. "Of course you can. I just *didn't*."

Griffin climbed the front steps, opened the door, and scooped up the small pile of mail that lay scattered on the mat. He opened the envelope that bore the logo of the Global Kennel Society, and pulled out a printed notice. "Luthor's confirmation for the big show," he announced. "All nice and official."

Ben tried to match his friend's smile. He was blown away that Operation Doggie Rehab had brought them to the point where Luthor had a chance to win at Global. It was always like that with Griffin's plans. They seemed like million-to-one shots. Yet suddenly, impossibly, the finish line beckoned, not too far out of reach.

But the Doberman was attracting more and more attention. They'd all be under a microscope at Global. If the word somehow trickled down to Ben's parents —

Frowning, he plucked a single piece of mail from Griffin's armload and held it so his friend could read the address:

LEX LUTHOR SAVANNAH SPRITZ-O-MATIC

"For Luthor?" Griffin mused.

Ben tore open the envelope and unfolded the contents.

quIt gLoBal wHilE tAilS aRe sTiLL WAggiNG
LuThoR wiLL LiVe tO tHanK yOU
tHis iS yOuR lASt WaRninG

"It's him again!" Ben was terrified. "The guy who put that note on Dmitri's car!"

"Or *her*," Griffin added, none too steady himself. "It could just as easily be a lady."

"Whoever it is, how did they find us in Cedarville?"

Griffin held up the confirmation form. "This is Luthor's address of record for the show. Anybody could get it from the Global Kennel Society."

"I'll bet it's Mr. Mustache," Ben accused. "Schroeder *owned* the Doberman breed until Luthor came along."

Griffin was thoughtful. "It could just as easily be that Nigel guy. He and Dmitri used to be archenemies back in the day."

"And Luthor beat him twice," Ben added breathlessly. "At group with one dog, and Show with another."

Griffin sighed. "The truth is, it could be anybody — even that sour-faced old bag who owns

Xerxes. Getting rid of Luthor opens things up for every dog at Global."

"Wouldn't it be a kicker if it turned out to be your girlfriend, Emma?"

Griffin reddened. "She would never do something like that."

"I think she'd do anything for her precious Jazzy."

"You're wrong," said Griffin, tight-lipped.

"Maybe we should take the letter to the police," Ben suggested.

"No police!" Griffin exclaimed. "The first thing they'd do is ask to talk to our parents."

"We can't just do *nothing*," Ben argued. "Someone's sending us threatening letters!"

"We'll tell Dmitri. He'll know how to handle it."

Luthor stood covered in suds in the claw-footed antique bathtub in his handler's second-floor apartment above the old Shaolin Palate. The Doberman maintained perfect stacking position as Dmitri scrubbed him down with a huge, long-handled push mop.

Since Dmitri's pinkie was not free to maintain

the dog's attention, he substituted his voice, sooth-ing yet in command: "Focus, Luthor . . . your mind is a laser beam . . . a concentrated point of pure light. . . ."

When the dog was fully lathered, Dmitri stripped down to a Speedo bathing suit, climbed into the tub beside his star pupil, and began to run the mop over himself.

The sound was distant, but unmistakable: *Crash!*

Breaking glass.

It disturbed Luthor's stance and galvanized the soaped-up Dmitri into sudden action. He was out of the tub and into the hallway in two strides of his long legs. Luthor was right behind him, paws skittering on the hardwood floor. To the Doberman's guard-dog instincts, a crash meant an intruder. And that was his business.

Dmitri started down the steps to the abandoned restaurant, but he was no match for Luthor's speed. The Doberman brushed past him and raced to the bottom. Powerful canine legs propelled the dog through the overturned chairs and rickety tables to the door that had once been the entrance to the Shaolin Palate. A fist-sized hole had been punched through the window, just below the

CONDEMNED sticker. On the floor in front of it lay a piece of raw steak.

Luthor started toward it.

"No-o-o!!"

Dmitri's commands were always quiet and calm, but this was practically a scream. Luthor stopped in his tracks long enough for the handler to hurl himself past the dog, shielding him from the door.

A jet of white foam that looked like shaving cream blasted through the hole in the glass. It caught Dmitri in midair, splattering over his face and bare chest. His size-fourteen foot came down on the meat, which slid out from under him. He hit the floor with a foundation-shaking thud.

On the other side of the door, partially hidden by the CONDEMNED sign, a black-clad figure turned and ran down the street.

Dmitri tried to scramble up to give chase. A stab of fire in his left knee told him that he would not be running anytime soon.

Slumping back in defeat, he took a whiff of the white foam that covered his face and upper body. "Hair remover," he diagnosed in a thready voice, and passed out cold.

22

By the time Griffin and Ben made it to the hospital, Dmitri was being wheeled out of Emergency by a young orderly in scrubs. Luthor trotted obediently behind the stretcher, following the raised pinkie, which protruded from the pale blue sheet covering the handler's long body.

"Dmitri!" Griffin called as they rushed over.

The big Russian's face was pale, but his eyes were even wilder than usual. Two-thirds of his beard and mustache had been burned away, revealing large patches of raw, irritated skin. Huge clumps of hair were gone, giving him the look of someone who had been attacked by a deranged barber.

"What happened?" Ben asked in awe.

"Dmitri has thwarted an attempt to remove Luthor from competition!" the patient declared in outrage.

"Somebody tried to kill him?" Horrified, Griffin thought back to the latest threatening message: *This is your last warning*, it had said. So the author had decided to back up those words with action.

"Far worse than that," the handler replied in disgust. "The coward attacked with hair remover — Nair, I believe."

Griffin's eyes traveled from the handler's patchy, uneven hair and red, inflamed skin to Luthor's shiny, perfect coat. If the depilatory foam had reached Luthor instead of the Russian, the Doberman would be in no condition to compete in a dog show — not with great patches of fur missing. He would have been knocked out as surely as Electra had been with her broken tail.

The orderly handed Griffin the leash. "You have to take the dog, kid. No animals in the operating room."

"Operating room?" Ben echoed. "He needs beard surgery?"

"Not his beard; his knee," the orderly informed

them. "The patient tore his ACL tripping on a steak."

The handler was tight-lipped. "Dmitri did not trip. Dmitri acted heroically as a human shield."

"It has to be repaired arthroscopically," the young man persisted. "And the dog isn't invited."

"I vouch for this dog's behavior with my very life!" the handler declared emotionally.

"The ambulance attendant said he was barking the neighborhood down."

"He had to alert the authorities to my predicament," Dmitri insisted. "With only a small hole in the door, he understood that great volume was required. If you do not see the genius in this, you are a fool."

The orderly was unimpressed. "Tell that to the doctor."

"Dmitri will tell it to the surgeon general himself!"

"Don't worry," Griffin soothed. "We'll look after Luthor."

"You will do more than that," the big Russian ordered. "You must take him home with you. Dmitri charges you with my brother's safety."

Ben emitted a cry that elicited a *shhh!* from every nurse up and down the hall. "But he's *good* with you! What if he goes back to his old self? He won't win Best in Show if he mauls all the judges!"

"Luthor is under attack," Dmitri reasoned. "Just as Electra was under attack when a dart was used to turn Luthor into a weapon against her. He is not safe in my home. Our enemy has already damaged one Best in Show."

"He's not safe at my house, either," Griffin exclaimed, worried. "The last note went to my address." He turned to Ben. "We'll keep him with us at your place."

"Are you nuts?" Ben blurted. "What about my parents? Luthor's not a turtle you can hide in a shoe box! My folks aren't blind, you know."

The orderly was growing impatient. "Somebody had better step up, because Mr. Trebezhov is going to be off his feet for the next six weeks."

"Six weeks?" squeaked Griffin. "But he's okay to handle Luthor in the dog show, right?"

"Absolutely — so long as he can do it sitting down."

Both boys pictured the job of a handler: walking with the dog; running with the dog; standing by the dog. There was no sitting.

Dmitri addressed Griffin. "*You* will handle Luthor at Global."

Griffin turned chalk white. "But it only works when you do it!"

"True, no one can replace Dmitri. But I will be there to oversee everything. Luthor will be fine. Make sure that you are also fine." With those words hanging in the antiseptic-smelling air, he was wheeled into surgery. As the doors swung shut, they heard him informing the doctor: "Dmitri is an organ donor. I have willed my pinkie to the Smithsonian."

Ben rounded on Griffin. "All right, Mr. Man-With-The-Plan. What has your precious plan got in mind for this?"

"It's not good," Griffin admitted.

"That's an understatement," Ben growled. "My mother notices when the ice maker gurgles in our fridge. You think she's going to miss Lex Luthor Savannah Spritz-o-matic?"

"We hid forty-two fugitive zoo animals," Griffin reminded him. "Surely we can hide one dog."

"We hid forty-two *small* zoo animals," Ben amended. "If there's a single word that doesn't apply to Luthor, it's *small*."

"It's a long train ride back to Cedarville. That'll give us time to do some planning."

Ben bit his lip. Another plan.

*   *   *

He did his best to tiptoe, but Mom heard him anyway.

"Benjamin — can I see you for a minute?"

Benjamin — never a good sign when she called him that.

He found her in the living room. "What's up, Mom?"

"I ran into Michelle, your swim coach. She tells me that you and Griffin haven't been showing up for class much lately."

"Really?" Ben bought himself a few precious seconds by pretending to be astounded. The boys had been pretty good about attending an early lesson before heading into Flushing every day during Luthor's training. Or so they'd thought. Apparently, their "occasional" absences had been piling up.

"I really don't mind if you miss a class or two," she went on pleasantly. "But it raises the question of what you'd been doing with all that time — Ben, are you listening to me?"

In fact, he was peering over her shoulder out the sheer curtains, where Griffin was sneaking across the lawn with Luthor on a leash. Ben followed their progress toward the basement window that they had chosen as an entry point. He lost them there. But a moment later, he heard a faint thud of boy and dog jumping to the concrete floor.

To cover up the commotion, he raced to the TV, switched it on, and cranked the volume up to 93. "You've got to see this, Mom. It's amazing!"

An Ex-Lax commercial blasted through the room.

"Turn that down!" Mrs. Slovak ordered.

"Wait! We're just getting to the good part!" What they were getting to, Ben knew, was where Griffin brought the dog out of the basement and up to the attic.

Ferret Face didn't appreciate the noise any more than Mom did. He burrowed in search of peace and quiet, pressing his head into Ben's armpit.

Mrs. Slovak hurried over and switched off the television. "I'm not watching a musical number about constipation. Now, look, if you don't want to swim, that's fine. Just let us know so we can stop paying for the lessons."

A soft *wump* from above told him that Griffin and Luthor had reached their destination, closing the trap door behind them.

"We'll do better," Ben assured her. And he intended to keep that promise — starting the day after the Global Kennel Society dog show.

If I live that long, he thought to himself.

To Luthor, the Slovaks' attic was a wonderful place. There was so much to investigate — endless boxes, golf clubs, camping equipment, a baby carriage, a rack of winter coats, antiquated vacuum cleaners, and scores of random objects just begging to be nuzzled and snuffled. Ben laid out an ancient sleeping bag for the Doberman's bed, but Luthor preferred to tunnel into a large rolled-up remnant of shag carpet.

Mrs. Slovak worked part-time as a real estate agent, so Griffin and Ben had plenty of opportunities to sneak Luthor in and out for exercise and to do his business. The boys had feared that, with Dmitri absent, Luthor's training would fade, and the old guard dog would return. But there was no sign of that. The big Doberman was acting like he really was a Best in Show winner. Even with Griffin as handler, he was stacking, gaiting, and responding to commands like a pro.

"That Dmitri must be some trainer" was

Griffin's opinion. "He might even be almost as good as *he* thinks he is."

"It's like Luthor's a totally different animal," Ben agreed. "I hope Savannah still likes him. He's not really her 'sweetie' anymore."

"Are you kidding?" Griffin scoffed. "He used to be a wild beast! Today he's a champion! He's a million times better."

"I didn't say he isn't *better*," Ben argued. "I just said he isn't Luthor."

Griffin wasn't buying it. "Just remember what would have happened if we hadn't sprung him from the pound. This new Luthor is a miracle — and we owe it all to Operation Doggie Rehab. And Dmitri."

The big Russian was out of the hospital now, prowling around $2^1/_2$ Packard Lane, his crutches thumping. The boys had his strict orders: Under no circumstances were they to bring the dog to visit him. His apartment was no longer safe. Their one job was to keep Luthor where he could not be found.

There was no question that their mysterious enemy was still looking to put the dog out of competition. On Thursday, another threatening note arrived at the Bing home.

```
LuThoR wAs lUcKy — tHis tIMe
wiTHdRaW fRom gLoBaL
nExT tiME i woN't MiSs
```

"Maybe *now* we should go to the police," Ben said reluctantly. "This proves that the author of the messages is the person who tried to attack Luthor and sprayed Dmitri by mistake."

"We will," Griffin promised. "After Global, when Operation Doggie Rehab is complete."

"It isn't just creepy messages with cutout letters anymore," Ben argued. "What happened to Dmitri was *assault*. This person is a criminal. We could end up dead — or at least bald!"

Griffin nodded slowly. "I see what you mean. This is getting too big for just two guys. I think we're going to have to expand the plan."

23

Most of the campers were asleep when the rickety yellow school bus exited the Long Island Expressway and headed north toward Cedarville. In the last row of seats, a heated argument was underway, conducted in whispers to avoid disturbing the other passengers.

"You were almost normal for an entire summer," accused Antonia Benson, whose nickname was Pitch. "And then you had to go and blow it on the very last night in the camp play."

"You can't expect me to do *Charlotte's Web* unless my character is believable," Logan said sulkily.

"You were playing a talking pig!" Pitch hissed. "How believable could it be?"

Logan was stubborn. "Wilbur wouldn't ask for special treatment just because he has connections with an influential spider. If the other pigs are going to be pork chops, he'd man up — I mean, *pig* up. He wouldn't be afraid to look death in the face. Sure, it's dark, but that's drama!"

Pitch was disgusted. "You didn't have to stab yourself on stage. All that blood —"

"It was ketchup."

"It was *gross*," Pitch amended.

The bus pulled over to the curb along Cedarville's main drag. "Last stop, you guys," announced the driver. "Everybody off."

The drowsy passengers began to rouse themselves.

Pitch swung a backpack over her shoulder and shuffled to the front. "It'll be good to see my folks. We're going rock climbing this weekend. Camp's fun, but it's too *flat*." The Bensons were avid mountaineers.

Logan was still on the previous conversation. "You can't just play a pig by crawling on all fours and saying 'oink.' You have to *be* the pig. When my drama club did *Animal Farm*, I contracted swine flu on purpose."

The door hissed open. At the front of the cluster of parents stood Griffin Bing.

Pitch didn't miss a beat. "Mom, you look different. Younger, somehow."

"We e-mailed your families that the bus was running late," Griffin explained. "That'll give us time to get you up to speed."

Logan was mystified. "Up to speed on what?"

Griffin smiled at them. "Welcome to Operation Watchdog."

PLAN OBJECTIVE: To keep Luthor SAFE at the Global Kennel Society show

THE TEAM:
GRIFFIN BING: Dog handler and Operation Manager. ASSIGNMENT: Put Luthor through his paces while coordinating team members via walkie-talkie.
BEN SLOVAK: Assistant handler and Luthor's shadow. ASSIGNMENT: Stick to Luthor like glue.
PITCH BENSON: Climber. ASSIGNMENT: Aerial surveillance from rafters of Manhattan Coliseum.
LOGAN KELLERMAN: Actor. ASSIGNMENT: Keep an eye on prime suspects by impersonating a dog owner.
LEX LUTHOR SAVANNAH SPRITZ-O-MATIC: Dog. ASSIGNMENT: Crush the competition and win Best in Show.

DISABLED LIST:

DMITRI TREBEZHOV: Inactive. Recovering from ACL surgery.

PRIME SUSPECTS:

NIGEL DIAMOND – Dmitri's nemesis

MR. MUSTACHE – Owner of Schroeder, rival Doberman

MRS. DEVLIN – Owner of Xerxes, Luthor's top competition

EMMA HIGHTOWER –

"That's not supposed to be there!" Griffin scratched out the last line, turning furious eyes on Ben. "I told you — Emma's not a suspect. She'd never hurt a dog!"

The first team meeting of Operation Watchdog was taking place in the Slovaks' backyard. Since Ben's parents were both at work, Luthor was with them, enjoying the sunny day after his long confinement in the attic.

"I forgot to tell you guys," Ben said to Pitch and Logan. "Griffin's in love now. And guess what — Luthor's in love with Griffin's girlfriend's poodle."

"She's not my girlfriend!" Griffin snapped. "She hates me now that Luthor beat Jasmine at Mid-Atlantic."

Pitch couldn't take her eyes off the Doberman. "I can't believe how different he is. I used to be afraid to turn my back on him! Now he's totally calm. This Dmitri guy must be really something."

"He's one of a kind," Ben agreed.

"I'm anxious to sink my teeth into a new role," said Logan. "Owner of a champion show dog. What's my motivation?"

"Just stay away from the ketchup," Pitch put in sourly.

"What kind of dog would my character own?" Logan persisted. "Big? Small? Maybe a rare breed — wouldn't that be something?"

"You're not going to have a dog with you," Ben explained patiently. "Posing as an owner is just your excuse for nosing around the Coliseum."

"It makes no dramatic sense," the young actor warned him.

"It doesn't have to make dramatic sense," Griffin insisted. "It has to make sense for the plan."

"What do you expect to do?" Pitch challenged. "*Rent* a dog?"

Logan folded his arms in front of him. "I can't work under these conditions."

With a sigh, Griffin reached up inside Ben's

T-shirt from the waist, drew out Ferret Face, and handed the writhing bundle of fur to Logan. "Now you've got a dog. It's a rare breed. *Very* rare."

"Wait a minute," Ben protested. "I need Ferret Face for my narcolepsy! What if I fall asleep in the middle of the show?"

"You'll have to tough it out," Griffin decided. "It's going to be crazy at the Coliseum — thousands of people, thousands of dogs. The noise alone will keep you awake."

"It doesn't work that way," Ben insisted. "Narcolepsy can get you any time, any place. And it's worse at times of stress."

"There's no reason to be stressed," Griffin soothed.

His friend turned an unhealthy shade of purple. "Are you out of your mind? Someone's out to attack Luthor and maybe us, too! We've lost our handler because he was shot with hair remover! My dad is complaining about squirrels in the attic! One of these days he's going to go up there and find a hundred-and-fifty-pound squirrel! If there was ever a time to be stressed, it's *right now*!"

Griffin put an arm around him. "We just have to focus. The only thing that matters is winning. The plan takes care of everything else. I just wish we had a way of catching the low-down skunk who ambushed Dmitri and Luthor."

They heard the click of the front gate, followed by a soft power hum. Around a hedge came a three-foot-high silver robot on caterpillar treads. Its rounded dome rotated slowly, and a light misting of water sprayed from a system of nozzles.

The group stared in amazement. Even Luthor broke his perfect stack to gawk. Ferret Face wriggled out of Logan's grasp and sought the shelter of Ben's shirt.

Melissa followed the robot, smiling with shy pride. "What do you think?"

Griffin almost exploded. "*The Spritz-o-matic!* You fixed it!"

"That's what you asked me to do."

"I asked you to put it back together!" Griffin sputtered. "You've got it *working*! It never worked before!"

"Oh," she said airily, "that was just because of a little glitch in the electronics. It took a while to figure out, but it's fine now. It even sprays, see? I filled the tank with water as a test, but it'll squirt anything."

Those three words — *it'll squirt anything* — brought the plan to perfect completion in Griffin's mind.

"It's okay, right?" Melissa added timidly. "You've got a weird look on your face."

"I think," said The Man With The Plan, "that I've figured out how we're going to catch the person who's trying to hurt Luthor."

24

In a small hotel room in Budapest, Mr. Bing shut the lid of his laptop computer. "Well, it's official. The Bulgarians have just placed an order for thirty Spritz-o-matics."

His wife switched off the TV, which was showing a rerun of *Seinfeld* dubbed in Hungarian. "Congratulations, dear."

"Thanks — I think," he said listlessly. "I'd be happier if it was for SmartPicks, or Rollo-Bushels, or even the vole traps. At least they work. What am I doing running around Europe when I should be in the garage, getting the bugs out of my prototype?"

"We've been over this a hundred times," Mrs. Bing soothed. "In order to be an inventor, you have to accept that selling is a part of it. The fact that it's a living is what makes it possible for you to continue to be creative."

"I want to go home," he said suddenly. "We only have one more meeting, and Luxembourg isn't a very big market. I'm calling the airline." He picked up his cell phone.

His wife sighed. "You're probably right. Griffin will be thrilled to see us come back early. He and Ben have no plans except a few swimming lessons. They're probably bored out of their minds. What could be worse than a whole summer with absolutely nothing to do?"

The annual Global Kennel Society competition was the Super Bowl of dog shows. Nearly three thousand animals from all fifty states, nine of ten Canadian provinces, and forty-seven countries around the world gathered in New York City to go snout-to-snout for the coveted top prize — Best in Show at the show of shows.

Every pet-friendly hotel room for fifty miles was full. Ultra-Hold Waterless Coat Spray was selling for sixty dollars per can on Third Avenue, higher inside the venue.

Traffic cops filled the streets around the sold-out Manhattan Coliseum, stopping cars for the parade of primped and coiffed canines and their hopeful owners and handlers. Taxis and limos waited as setters and retrievers marched across the road, tails in the air. The assortment of dogs was dizzying — whippets and Akitas, Weimaraners and borzois, bullmastiffs and bichon frises, Lhasa apsos and wirehaired pointing griffons. Their owners were an even more diverse group — from amateur mom-and-pop teams who had scrimped and saved for the trip to New York, to billionaires arriving in private helicopters and chauffeured Bentleys. Slick professional handlers sized up the competition with narrowed expert eyes. There could be no question that this was the big one. Even the smoggy city air felt electric — charged particles dancing in anticipation.

Floodlights made the Coliseum's atrium as bright as any Hollywood soundstage. Video cameras and microphones pointed and waved in all directions as reporters interviewed owners, handlers, judges, Global officials, vendors, and security guards. A few even tried to coax a woofed comment from the dogs themselves.

As soon as Griffin led Luthor through the entranceway, a cry went up.

"There they are!"

The stampede toward them seemed almost

liquid — eddies and currents in a swirling sea of people. In a heartbeat, Griffin was staring at a dozen lenses. Pencils poised over notepads as the questions came at rapid-fire pace.

"Did the Doberman attack Electra to clear his own path to Global?"

"Is it true that the dog broke Dmitri Trebezhov's legs?"

"Do you know that Lady Gaga friended Luthor on Facebook?"

"What's your explanation for Luthor's extraordinary size?"

"Well — uh —" Griffin felt his head spinning. Which question did you try to answer when they were all coming at the same time? To his dismay, the crush of reporters had stopped his progress and was pushing him up against a mirrored wall. He didn't mind so much for himself, but Luthor was getting edgy. And that would be bad news all around.

The crutch came out of nowhere. It knocked the microphone clean out of one reporter's hand and jostled a video camera, brushing back the onslaught of press. Into the open space thumped the towering figure of Dmitri Trebezhov. He looked even more bizarre than usual in his orange DayGlo.

Although he had trimmed his hair and beard, it was impossible to hide the damage done by the Nair attack.

"No comment!" he announced, and fixed the press with such a glare that they stepped aside to let Luthor and Griffin through.

Finally, one man worked up the courage to ask, "Dmitri — how did you get injured?"

"Dmitri is not injured," came the growled reply. "My new hobby is limping."

"How can Luthor win without you?" asked the woman from the *Canine Chronicle.*

"Because he is the best dog by many levels of magnitude."

With Dmitri leading, Griffin and Luthor made their way toward the benching area.

"Thanks," Griffin told the hobbled handler. He studied his black sneakers. "Ben and I are really sorry you got hurt. We were just trying to help Luthor. In a million years we never thought anything bad would happen to you."

"Dmitri will forgive you," the big Russian offered generously, "*if* you can bring my brother to his destiny."

Griffin gulped. There was a moment in every plan when somebody had to come up big. Now it

would be his turn. Luthor was good enough —
he had proven that in New Jersey. But there his
leash had rested in the hand of the greatest trainer
in history.

When Lex Luthor Savannah Spritz-o-matic got
in front of the judges today, the hand on that leash
would belong to The Man With The Plan.

The instant her fingers touched the steel util-
ity ladder, Pitch Benson knew she was in her
element.

Climbing — turning the world vertical. There
was nothing quite like it.

It had been simple enough to sneak into the
main arena, which was deserted except for a few
technicians setting up the TV cameras and control
booth. With the huge arc lights off, she had crept
through the shadows unnoticed. Now, on the ladder, she was doing her best to look like she
belonged. After all, who would scale a hundred-
thirty-foot ladder without a very good reason?

Pitch had a reason, but it wasn't anything
Coliseum security would have approved of. How
many times had she done crazy things like this for
Griffin and his stupid plans? Operation Watchdog!

What next? But if Luthor's life and the Drysdale family's future really were at stake, then she was all for it.

And anyway, it's good to be climbing again.

At the top, she swung a leg over the rail and effortlessly hoisted herself onto the platform. The fact that she was twelve stories above the hard floor worried her not at all. Pitch had been in similar positions on mountains, cliffs, and crags all across the continent.

She plugged the earpiece attachment into the walkie-talkie in her jacket pocket. "Griffin, do you read me?"

"Loud and clear," came the reply. "Are you in position?"

"Yes and no," Pitch informed him. "I'm about eight feet below the Coliseum ceiling. But I'm up too high for a good look at what's going on in the ring."

"Any chance of getting a little lower?" he asked.

"Not unless I can levitate."

"There must be someplace," Griffin insisted. "Maybe another spot in the arena?"

Pitch looked around. Her platform was actually a long maintenance catwalk to the very center of the Coliseum. There another ladder led down to the enormous high-tech scoreboard, which was suspended about forty feet below the roof.

"Jackpot," she said.

As security chief of the Manhattan Coliseum, Marcus Hamlin thought he'd seen it all, from the escaped convict posing as a trapeze artist at the Big Apple Circus to the rock band that smuggled a 750-pound black bear onstage.

Yet never had he encountered anything quite like the mysterious, three-foot-high device the stringy-haired girl was trying to bring into the Global Kennel Society show.

"What is it — some kind of fancy blow-dryer?" He tipped up her hand truck and examined the base. "Are these caterpillar tracks? It looks like a miniature tank."

Melissa was tongue-tied behind her curtain of hair. She had only recently developed the courage to hold conversations with her classmates. Adults were out of the question — especially adults in uniform. "It's for our dog," she managed, but so quietly that he was unable to hear her over the crowd noise.

"What was that? Speak up!" Hamlin prompted.

A Global official came over to investigate. "What seems to be the problem here?"

"I can't let her inside," the security chief explained, "until I know what this contraption is for. And she can't seem to tell me."

The official examined the device, running a hand over the smooth, stainless-steel casing. Her fingers stopped on the engraved name, and she took a closer look.

SPRITZ-O-MATIC

"Spritz-o-matic," the woman repeated. "Is this for Lex Luthor Savannah Spritz-o-matic?"

Melissa nodded vigorously, although her eyes made no appearance from their hiding place behind her hair.

Hamlin was mystified. "And exactly what is that supposed to mean?"

"Lex Luthor Savannah Spritz-o-matic is the dog who brought the great Dmitri Trebezhov out of retirement," the official explained. "He's the most exciting Doberman to come along in fifty years."

"So I can go in?" Melissa barely whispered.

"Not till I know what I'm looking at," the chief insisted.

The official overruled him. "If this is good enough for Dmitri Trebezhov, it's good enough for me. I vouch for this young lady personally."

Logan Kellerman was deep in character when he approached the man with the mustache in the benching area. "Beautiful dog," he complimented. "What do you think of mine?" He adjusted the blanket in his arms to reveal the gray, needle-nosed features of Ferret Face.

The man recoiled. "Holy hamburgers, what do you call *that*?"

"He's a Manchurian weasel terrier," Logan explained. "Not yet recognized by the Kennel Society. The breed is under review for next year."

The man's eyes narrowed. "Are you sure that's a dog?"

The actor had prepared for exactly that question. "Weasel terriers date back before the building of the Great Wall of China . . ."

He felt a tap on his shoulder. Ben.

"Not now," Logan hissed. "I'm acting."

"But you've got the wrong guy."

"You told me the man with the mustache," Logan insisted.

"Yeah, the mustache and the *Doberman*," Ben whispered. "This is a Labrador retriever." He pointed to Mr. Mustache, who stood with Schroeder a few aisles over. *"Him."*

Logan sniffed, annoyed. "An actor can only be as good as his director." To the retriever owner he said, "Thanks for nothing!" Then he spun on his heel and headed in the direction of Schroeder and his master.

A nervous yawn escaped Ben, and he dug his fingernails into his arm until the pain had brought him back to alertness. He couldn't allow himself to fall asleep.

Not now.

25

Luthor's stunning victory in New Jersey allowed him to skip the class-level competition for Dobermans. He relaxed in his kennel while Dmitri read him another chapter from *Lassie Come-Home*. The benching area at Global was a madhouse. There were three times as many dogs as at Mid-Atlantic, and large numbers of handlers and support staff. Unlike the outdoor shows, this was a confined, overcrowded space. It was much more distracting for the animals, yet Luthor seemed perfectly calm listening to Dmitri's gruff but somehow soothing voice.

Griffin wished with all his heart that he could be soothed, too. He was about to handle a major contender at the biggest show of the year. If that didn't count as trial by fire, nothing would.

To divert his mind, he tried to assist Melissa, who was wiring the Spritz-o-matic to the door of their kennel. That was their strategy to trap the person who was out to harm Luthor: Any attempt to open the latch would activate the spray function, covering the guilty party in fluorescent green dye.

"I've set the motion lock on the robot so it won't move," she explained. "When you want to take Luthor out, remember to turn off the Spritz-o-matic. If you forget, you're green. Got it?"

"Won't Luthor get sprayed, too?" Griffin asked, worried.

The shy girl shook her head. "I've disabled the nozzles that point in his direction. He'll be fine."

Griffin nodded tensely. "The plan is totally in place." He spoke into his walkie-talkie. "Control to lookout. Pitch — any sign of our suspects?"

"Check," the climber reported from her perch high up in the arena. "I'm on top of the scoreboard, looking straight down at that Nigel guy."

"Are you sure it's him?" Griffin asked.

"You can't miss this creep," Pitch assured him. "You can smell the hair oil from here. This is the third time he's been in the ring. How many dogs does he have?"

"He's a factory," Griffin told her. "He'll be hard to keep track of, but do your best. Control out."

Someone behind him said softly, "Is it okay if we set up here?"

Griffin would have recognized that voice anywhere. He whirled to find himself looking into the sea-green eyes of Emma Hightower. "Yeah!" he exclaimed too eagerly. Then, remembering how angry she'd been at the end of Mid-Atlantic, he added. "Um — are you sure you want to be so close to us?"

She nodded and set Jasmine's kennel down next to the spot where Dmitri's crutches leaned against a pillar. "Everyone's talking about what happened to Mr. Trebezhov. The word is that you're going to handle Luthor."

"Or Luthor's going to handle me," Griffin tried to joke.

She studied the floor. "I'm sorry I said such mean things about you and Luthor. I was just being a sore loser. I thought Jazzy had a real shot at Best in Show."

Griffin watched as the poodle hunkered down in her cage, completely absorbed in Dmitri's voice reading from *Lassie Come-Home*. She and Luthor seemed to be comfortably aware of each other.

"I understand," Griffin told her. "It's a high-pressure business."

The PA system crackled to life. "The Doberman breed judging will commence in five minutes."

Griffin squared his shoulders. "Speaking of pressure . . ."

"You'll do fine," Emma soothed. "Luthor's awesome. He deserves all the attention he's getting."

To walk from the drab, cluttered benching area into the brilliantly lit arena was like entering an alien landscape. The stands were packed, and thousands of camera flashes made them seem to glitter. As Griffin stepped onto the green carpet of the ring, he looked up, hoping to catch a glimpse of Pitch peering out over the side of the scoreboard. He couldn't spot her, but it was nice to know she was up there, rooting for him. He did notice Dmitri inconveniencing the entire front row of the grandstand as he thumped his way to his seat. Ben was with him, looking on anxiously. Melissa was stationed back at the Spritz-o-matic, and Logan was circulating with his Manchurian weasel terrier. It was the plan, unfolding in its complex glory. But in a spot like this, Griffin was too nervous to appreciate it.

Everything had come down to this: Would Luthor perform for anyone but Dmitri? They were minutes away from finding out.

At last, the moment of truth arrived, and the judge's hands were on Luthor. Griffin could envision the nightmare scenario as clear and as large as a horror movie in IMAX: Luthor, recoiling from the touch; the bark of outrage; the snap of sharp teeth; the disqualification; the disgrace. . . .

When there was no sound, he dared to open his eyes. He had never seen Luthor so totally serene. At that moment, he knew that the big guy could do it. Luthor was going all the way.

And when the gaiting and stacking were through, and the judge announced, "Number forty-one," Griffin didn't even have to check his armband to confirm it. Luthor had won Best of Breed.

The roar of approval that rang out in the arena sealed the victory. The most knowledgeable crowd in the dog world had taken its first look at Lex Luthor Savannah Spritz-o-matic, the next superstar of the Global Kennel Society.

In the stands, Ben was on his feet, screaming himself hoarse. Even Dmitri raised a crutch in triumph, knocking a very stylish hat off the head of a well-dressed lady.

From the walkie-talkie in his pocket, he could hear Pitch screaming from somewhere above. "What just happened? What just happened? It's good, right?"

He raised his arm, flashing a triumphant thumbs-up in the direction of the scoreboard.

A few of the other handlers came forward to offer their congratulations, but Griffin could feel resentment radiating from Mr. Mustache. This meant an early exit for Schroeder.

Ben caught up with Griffin and Luthor at the tunnel that led to the benching area. Logan was waiting for them there. Ferret Face tried to make the leap to his owner, but Logan held him tightly.

"Luthor won Best of Breed!" Griffin announced, delighted.

Logan's mind was elsewhere. "These people are total snobs," he announced, lip curling. "Everybody says there's no such breed as a Manchurian weasel terrier. Like they're such big experts!"

"They *are* experts," Griffin reminded him. "And there *is* no such breed as a Manchurian weasel terrier. Get a grip."

Logan sighed patiently. "An actor has to immerse himself in a role."

"Yeah, but he doesn't have to do it with some other guy's ferret," Ben muttered.

Dmitri came up behind them. "Congratulations, my brother," he said to Luthor. "And I am truly sorry."

As they started along the aisle to their spot, Griffin waved to Melissa. "Good news — we advanced!"

It was only then that he noticed the expression on her face. Her curtain of hair was parted, revealing skin that was chalk white, her eyes haunted.

"What's wrong?"

"I — I only went to the bathroom. I was gone less than a minute, and when I got back —" She indicated a piece of paper taped to the top of Luthor's kennel.

sTAy hoMe tOMorRow oR
wHaTever hApPenS wiLL bE
bY yOUr oWn HaNd

Griffin turned to Emma, who was fluffing Jasmine's white pouf with a tiny pick. "Did you see anyone come near our kennel?"

"No, but I've been busy with Jazzy," she replied. "What's going on?"

"Somebody's out to get Luthor," Griffin told her. He turned to the others. "It can't be Mr. Mustache. He was in the ring with me."

"Unless he hired someone else to do his dirty work for him," Melissa put in.

"What about that Nigel guy?" Ben suggested. "He doesn't handle a Doberman."

"Maybe my mother saw something," Emma said helpfully. She waved over to the next aisle. "Mom, can you come here for a minute?"

Mrs. Hightower detached herself from a conversation and picked her way through the tight rows to her daughter.

Griffin stared at her, first in recognition, then in shock. His mind took him back to the Cedarville Mall on that fateful day of Luthor's rampage and Electra's injury. Right before the chaos, they had found themselves standing right next to *this lady* — a tall red-haired woman in a silver raincoat!

He was such a natural planner himself that when he glimpsed the enemy's plan, he recognized it at once. It played itself out in his brain like a movie: *Mrs. Hightower, a dog expert, instantly*

*recognizes Luthor's potential to create havoc. She
reaches into the pocket of her raincoat, drawing
out the dart gun. . . .*

"It was *you*!" he accused Emma. "You knew
Jasmine could never beat Electra. So you sent your
mother to cause a riot at the Cedarville Mall! And
she used poor Luthor to do it!"

Mrs. Hightower was thunderstruck. "Emma
wasn't even at that mall appearance," she
exclaimed. "I just happened to be there shopping."

"Exactly what are you trying to say?" Emma
demanded.

"I'm not *trying* to say anything; I'm saying it!
Your mother shot Luthor with a dart and made him
injure Electra. And now that *he* looks like a winner, you're after him, too! You've been threatening
us — you had the nerve to do it right here! You put
Dmitri in the hospital, and you almost sprayed
Luthor with Nair — all so Jasmine can win a stupid dog show!"

Waves of red-hot anger were radiating from
Emma. "There was always something about you,
Griffin Bing, that I couldn't quite put my finger on!
Now I know what it is! You're a moron!"

"Yeah, well, this moron is breaking up with
you!" Griffin snarled. "We're finished!"

"I take it back!" she shrilled. "You're not a moron — you're *completely insane!*"

"We'll see who's insane tomorrow when Luthor wipes up the arena with that useless puffball of yours!" Griffin shot back.

Shaking with rage, Emma grabbed Jasmine's leash and stormed away from them. Her mother followed, turning back to warn Griffin, "You stay away from my daughter!"

Dmitri put a large hand on Griffin's shoulder. "You are man of passion, my young friend."

"Do you think they really did it?" Ben asked his friend.

"It is of little importance," said the big Russian.

Griffin was astonished. "Are you kidding? They put you in the hospital! They broke Electra's tail! They got our friend's family sued for seven million dollars!"

"Details." The handler shrugged it off. "It will all be settled tomorrow on the only battlefield that matters — in the ring."

26

Ben awoke early the next morning and hurried downstairs to a sight that very nearly laid him out flat. His father, still in pajamas and bathrobe, sat at the kitchen table, leafing through a copy of the yellow pages.

"Dad — why aren't you getting ready for work?"

"I took a half day," his father replied in a haggard tone. "There's definitely some kind of animal in our attic. But I'm afraid to go and look myself — the last thing we need is a big, rabid raccoon getting loose. It's time to call in a professional."

Ben fought off a rush of panic. Global was a two-day event, with all the important stuff — the group judging and Best in Show — coming toward the end.

How's Luthor supposed to win if we can't get him out of the house?

"Maybe we should just — you know — wait," Ben wheedled. "If the animal could squeeze in, it could also squeeze out, right? Maybe it'll just leave."

Mr. Slovak shook his head. "Too risky. What if it's a pregnant female? Next thing you know, there's a whole metropolis up there."

By the time Ben was back upstairs breaking the news to Griffin, he was gray in the face. "What are we going to do?"

Griffin looked thoughtful. "Maybe it wouldn't be such a bad idea to confess. One way or another, this thing ends today. We won't be able to keep it a secret forever. Especially if Luthor becomes the most famous dog in the world."

Ben was against it. "You don't know my folks. They could be so mad we've been lying to them all summer that they won't let us go. Can you imagine losing Global because we don't show up? Dmitri'll kill us! *I'll* kill us!"

"Good point." Griffin didn't panic. The Man With The Plan never did. It was a waste of good effort when you could be finding a solution. He grabbed the phone and dialed the Benson home.

Pitch answered. "Jeez, Griffin. You mind if I

finish my cornflakes before I go use the Coliseum scoreboard as a hammock?"

"First things first," he told her. "We've got a problem."

She was instantly on board. The team was always up for a challenge. "What can I do?"

"Remember that mountain rescue course you took last summer . . . ?"

The climbing harness fit easily around Luthor's midsection, and the nylon alpine cords were rated at one thousand pounds plus. Griffin, Pitch, Melissa, and Logan were assembled in the attic — more than enough manpower to support the Doberman's weight. Ben was poised on the back patio, ready to receive the package and smuggle it out of the yard.

When Luthor eased over the windowsill, he looked twice as big as usual, and three times as heavy. His trip down was a little choppy, but the Doberman was alert enough to use his big paws to cushion his body from scraping along the aluminum siding. Through the kitchen window, Ben could see the back of his father's head. Dad was still poring over the yellow pages, completely unaware that a hundred-and-fifty-pound animal was being lowered out of his attic not six feet behind him.

"Easy, boy. Don't be scared," Ben whispered as Luthor approached the ground.

Their biggest fear was that Luthor would be so traumatized at being dangled in thin air that he would forget his training and revert to his old self. But as the Doberman touched down, Ben saw nothing but cool serenity in the dark eyes.

Dmitri really is a genius, he thought to himself. *Nothing could get a rise out of this dog.*

He undid the harness and signaled to Griffin in the attic window. Ropes and harness were drawn back up the side of the house, disappearing from sight.

Inside the kitchen, Mr. Slovak found the listing for the company he'd been looking for. He reached for the telephone.

Electra the beagle, the most decorated dog in Global Kennel Society history, sat on a satin cushion in the Coliseum, watching the competitors arrive for day two. Until a new Best in Show was selected later that afternoon, she was still the reigning champion.

Whether or not she recalled her own glories in this ring was anybody's guess. But she seemed animated and interested as the contestants walked past on the way to the benching area. Only once did her perfect composure desert her — when the top Doberman appeared. He made her nervous — filling her with the sense that something bad was about to happen.

Her owner soothed her with a calm he himself did not feel.

If it hadn't been for Lex Luthor Savannah Spritz-o-matic, his Electra would be in the ring at this very moment, instead of in the stands.

27

The silver raincoat wheeled around, and Mrs. Hightower turned furious eyes on Logan. "Will you stop following me?"

Logan held out a clipboard. "Will you sign this petition to add Manchurian weasel terriers to the breed list for next year's show?"

She slapped it away. "Don't think I don't recognize you from yesterday! You tell your friend Griffin to stop hassling me, my daughter, and our dog, or he will hear from my lawyer!"

As she stormed away, Logan spoke into his walkie-talkie. "Griffin, the role isn't working for me. It's one thing when the audience doesn't applaud, but she's threatening to sue."

"Stick to her anyway," Griffin ordered. "The working group is on next. We can't let her get a shot at Luthor when we're so close."

*   *   *

Cleopatra's home at the lake house was the wood box on the screen porch. It was Savannah's job to line it with fresh newspapers every day. This morning, though, the capuchin was frantic — gibbering, chattering, and slapping at Savannah's hand as she tried to smooth the paper out. When Savannah attempted to put down a second layer, the monkey grabbed it and tossed it over the rail.

Savannah was attuned to her animals' moods. "What is it, Cleo? What are you trying to tell me?"

Cleopatra picked up another sheet and pushed it at her owner and friend.

"I don't see what you're —" Her eyes fell on a murky photograph of a dog barely visible behind a large prize ribbon. The headline read:

OVERSIZED DOBERMAN BEATS ODDS TO QUALIFY FOR GLOBAL

METUCHUN, NJ — The Mid-Atlantic Kennel Society is still reeling from the unexpected Best in Show victory by a previously unknown and very unlikely winner, a Dobie that tips the scales forty pounds heavier than the breed standard. Handled by the great Dmitri Trebezhov, returned from retirement . . .

After that, the page was torn. She searched for the rest of the article, but came up empty. She stared at her monkey. Did Cleo think that was a picture of *Luthor*? Luthor was missing — or worse. He certainly wasn't winning prizes at dog shows, handled by Dmitri Trebezhov himself!

The last thing Savannah wanted to do was to follow this year's Global event. The mere thought of dogs made her weak in the knees these days. You had to be a hermit not to know that the big show was going on at the Manhattan Coliseum. But she had vowed not to watch one second of it, certain it would be too painful.

Now, though, her curiosity got the better of her, and she ran to the television. A large Doberman was still a painful memory, but how could she pass up the chance to see Dmitri Trebezhov in action?

She switched on the set. A moment later, she was leaning back into the sofa cushions, more shocked than she could have imagined. There, larger than life on the screen, was Luthor — *her* Luthor! And he wasn't abandoned or anything horrible like that. He was the most beautiful sight she'd ever seen in her life — proud and perfect at the very epicenter of the dog world.

How was this possible? How? Was she dreaming?

Then the camera pulled back to reveal the handler. It was not the legendary Dmitri Trebezhov.

It was Griffin Bing.

"Da-a-a-ad!!!"

Mr. Drysdale ran into the room. "What is it, honey? What's wrong?" His eyes fell on the screen. "Whoa — isn't that —?"

"It's Luthor! Somehow Griffin saved him!"

Her father was thunderstruck. "I can't believe it. When I spoke to him, he didn't say anything about entering a dog show."

"What?" Savannah was beside herself. "You spoke to Griffin? Why didn't you tell me?"

"He wasn't making sense," Mr. Drysdale tried to explain. "He told me a cockamamie story about how Luthor was innocent, and he only went berserk at the mall because somebody shot him with a dart. You were already so upset. I didn't want to get your hopes up on the say-so of a flake like Griffin Bing."

Savannah drew herself up to her full height. "Griffin is not a flake! He is The Man With The Plan, and his plan rescued Luthor from the pound! He is the greatest friend anybody ever had, and as soon as we get to the Coliseum, I'm going to tell him so!"

"The Coliseum?" her father repeated. "Honey, be reasonable. New York is four hours away."

On the TV, the working group judge had reached his decision. "The Doberman," he announced to thunderous applause.

"Start the car!"

To the Bings, the smog of New York was a beautiful sight because it meant they were almost home. Even the traffic jam on the Long Island Expressway was bearable because it was bringing them — bumper to bumper — back to Cedarville. At last, their van was navigating the familiar streets of their neighborhood. They drove not to their own block, but to the Slovaks'. After weeks in Europe, what they missed most was Griffin.

A large panel truck was parked in the driveway: BRICKHAUS NUISANCE WILDLIFE REMOVAL.

"Uh-oh," said Mr. Bing. "Looks like Griffin spent his big sleepover up to his ears in squirrels."

His wife shuddered. "I hope not."

They walked around the side of the house in time to hear Mr. Slovak exclaim, "What do you mean, there's nothing up there? I'm not crazy! I heard an animal moving around!"

"I said there's nothing up here *now*," Mr. Brickhaus called down from the attic. "I didn't say there never was. It climbed right up the wall and in this window. Look at the paw prints on the siding."

"That's impossible," protested Mr. Slovak. "How can an animal walk up a wall?"

"With this." The nuisance wildlife specialist dangled a climbing harness over the sill.

Mr. Bing spoke up. "Sorry to interrupt, Pete. I know you've got trouble. Do you know where the boys are?"

"Oh, welcome back," Mr. Slovak greeted him. "Sorry, I'm kind of distracted. Try the Bensons'. Pitch is home from camp."

But at the Benson house, they were told that Pitch was out, too — at Melissa's. There, Mrs. Dukakis directed them to the Kellermans'. And Mrs. Kellerman assured them that Logan was at Ben's.

Back in the car, Mrs. Bing was uneasy. "You know, my spider sense is tingling. Weird trouble at Pete's, and the kids using one another as excuses. If this isn't a plan, I'll eat my luggage."

"Let's go home," Mr. Bing suggested. "Maybe they're all hiding out at our place."

They parked in the driveway and Mrs. Bing unlocked the front door. "Griffin? Anybody here?"

The house was deserted.

Mr. Bing punched in the code to open the garage door. He let out a gasp as if he'd been punched in the stomach when he took in the wreckage of his workshop. But his horror at the mess disappeared in an instant when he looked for the prototype of his latest invention.

"The Spritz-o-matic!" he wheezed. "It's gone!"

"We've been robbed!" his wife shrilled. "And the thieves ransacked the place!"

A determined expression replaced the anguish on Mr. Bing's face. "They won't get away with it!" he all but snarled. "I built a GPS into the Spritz-o-matic so you can track it in the orchard." He threw open the door of the van and pulled his laptop out of his suitcase. "I can pinpoint its location!"

Mrs. Bing peered over her husband's shoulder as he pounded the keyboard. "New York City? What's it doing in New York City?"

"The corner of Pitt Street and Third Avenue!" he declared, leaping behind the wheel. "Get in the car!"

"Shouldn't we call the police?" his wife asked anxiously.

"We can do that on the way!"

And he left the driveway, burning rubber.

28

As the afternoon progressed in the Manhattan Coliseum, the champions of 167 breeds marched into the ring to be judged. One by one, the group champions were selected — the dogs that would compete for the ultimate prize.

Luthor came from the working group, Xerxes from the toys. Nigel Diamond's greyhound won the hounds again. The Welsh springer spaniel from the sporting group had crossed the ocean from England after winning every major competition in Europe. The terrier was a Lakeland, considered the number-one dog in the American heartland. The dog who had traveled the farthest to come to Global was the herding choice, an Australian shepherd, who had flown first class all the way from Brisbane.

Non-sporting was last. Griffin and Ben rooted wholeheartedly for Jasmine to lose. Yet the sheer training and quality of Emma's poodle carried the day.

When the seven finalists were set, a tense quiet fell over the arena. It had been good sport and good fun up until this point. But the coming hours would select Best in Show at Global, the pinnacle of canine achievement. The winner would be top dog in the world — with endorsement deals and breeding fees in the millions of dollars. Smiles were replaced by game faces. Warmth cooled. Friendships were put on the back burner. This was big, big business.

In the benching area, Dmitri was feeding Luthor ziti noodles through the grille of the kennel. "If there are to be dirty tricks," he warned the team, "they will come now. Be watchful."

Griffin nodded gravely. "We all know Luthor can take Best in Show. But if something goes wrong and he doesn't, *please* don't let that stupid poodle win. I couldn't stand to see Emma and her rotten mother happy after what they did to us."

Pitch spoke via walkie-talkie. "If I don't get something to eat, I'm going to fall off the scoreboard and flatten a couple of the contestants. Anybody want to meet at the snack bar?"

"I'm pretty hungry, too," put in Melissa timidly.

"We should all get some food," Griffin advised. "We want to be sharp when Luthor goes for the gusto."

Leaving Ben and Logan in the benching area with Luthor, the others headed for the concession stands. Dmitri had parting words for his star pupil. "You will win, of course. I'm sorry. It is unavoidable."

Ben watched them walk away. "You know," he said, turning to the dog, "in September when my teacher makes us do essays on 'How I Spent My Summer Vacation,' I'm going to write about this, and probably get sent to a psychiatrist."

A droplet of drool fell off the end of Luthor's long tongue.

Ben shook his head. "You may be a champion, but you have no idea what it's like to be best friends with The Man With The Plan."

The yawn came so suddenly that it shocked him. *Oh, no! Not here!*

He stood up. "Logan!"

Through the crowd, he could see the actor still trying to convince people about his "rare breed."

"Logan, I need Ferret Face right now!"

Had he actually managed to say that out loud? It felt more like a dream.

And anyway, it was already too late.

He slumped back onto the folding chair, sound asleep.

A shadowy figure dressed entirely in black moved soundlessly around the edge of the benching area. Could it be true? There was Lex Luthor Savannah Spritz-o-matic, almost entirely unattended. The youth who was supposed to be watching him had dozed off. The other boy — the dingbat — was at the center of a crowd, still trying to pass off his ferret as a dog. There would never be a better chance than right now.

Today the job could not be left to anything as unreliable as hair remover. It would be done the way it had happened at the Cedarville Mall. One quick dart. A berserk dog could not even be presented for judging. And this time, Dmitri Trebezhov was not here to get his big clumsy body in the way. This shot would be fired from point-blank range.

As the figure approached, a long-fingered white hand drew the small dart gun out of the trench coat pocket. The guard dog in Luthor sensed danger. He scrambled to his feet but found himself locked in, helpless. The pistol aimed at his long flank.

"No-o-o-o!!"

Logan came sprinting through the dense crowd, bowling people over. *"Get away from —"* His foot caught in the power cable of a hand dryer, and his run became a flight parallel to the floor. As he fell, the baby blanket was tossed from his arms, sending Ferret Face hurtling through the air. The terrified little animal struck the dart gun just as the trigger was pulled. His weight threw off the aim, and the shot missed Luthor, the dart bouncing harmlessly against the terrazzo.

Logan came down hard on the kennel, popping the door open. This sprung Melissa's trip wire, and the Orchard Spritz-o-matic whirred to life. The first blast of bright green dye covered the shadowy figure from head to toe.

The dart gun clattered to the floor, taking Ferret Face with it. The frightened creature scrambled for safety. He ran straight up Ben's pant leg, under his belt, and into his shirt.

As the attacker turned to flee, a high-stepping shoe bumped into the Spritz-o-matic, knocking off the motion catch. With nothing holding it back, the device began to move, its nozzle heads rotating, spraying dye in all directions. Logan, dazed on the floor, was splattered. Ben, still asleep, took a face-full. A fine spray marked Luthor's hindquarters as he pushed his way out of the kennel.

To the Spritz-o-matic, this was not the benching area of the finest dog show on the planet. It was an orchard, and the obstacles it was encountering were fruit trees. It did what it was programmed to do — bounce off, find open ground, and spray. Panic broke out among the owners and handlers. The dogs weren't thrilled about it, either. The sudden cold spray plus the panic from the humans was enough to erase tens of thousands of hours of painstaking training. The stampede to get away from the wandering robot had people and animals tripping over one another and their kennels and equipment. Stacks of gear tumbled. Bottles of cosmetics shattered. Doggie treats littered the floor.

Nuzzled in Ben's shirt, Ferret Face performed his sole function. He delivered a wake-up nip to his sleeping master.

Ben returned to consciousness to find himself surrounded by total chaos. He gawked. He goggled. There was a full-blown riot in the benching area.

Everything was stained with green. Even *he* was green!

What did I sleep through — World War Three?

He looked around desperately. Luthor was gone; the Spritz-o-matic prototype was gone; Logan was laid out on the floor. Screams and crashes echoed all around him.

There was only one thing to do: Find The Man With The Plan.

Griffin and Melissa, their arms laden with hot dogs and drinks for the team, reentered the arena from the concession stands, heading to the tunnel that led to the benching area.

When the crazed green person came pounding toward them, they stopped and stared. The significance of the color struck Melissa first.

"He's green!" she exclaimed.

"He's *Ben*!" Griffin added.

"Don't you get it?" Melissa insisted. "The Spritz-o-matic's gone off! Somebody must have attacked Luthor!"

They dropped the food and ran. Griffin grabbed his friend by the shirt, staining his own fingers. "What happened? Who set off the robot?"

Ben's eyes were haunted. "I didn't see! I was asleep!"

"Where's Luthor?" Melissa probed. "Is he all right?"

Ben could only shrug helplessly.

Griffin reached for his walkie-talkie. "Pitch — we've lost Luthor. Any sign of him from up there?"

"Hold on. I'm just getting back." There was a long pause as the climber scanned the crowded Coliseum from her perch atop the scoreboard. "I don't see him," she reported finally. "But listen — when the cage opened, did the Spritz-o-matic shoot anybody?"

Griffin took in Ben's fluorescent features. "Big-time. Why?"

"Because there's a totally green person running through the seats."

Griffin stared. Pitch was right. Across the arena, a smallish, black-clad figure — liberally spattered with green — was ascending the grand-stand toward an upper side exit.

He took off in pursuit. "Find Luthor!" he tossed over his shoulder. "And somebody shut down the Spritz-o-matic!"

"But it's gone, too!"

Griffin stopped on a dime. "Don't tell me that!

Please don't tell me that!" He was torn in two. They had the culprit, caught red-handed — or at least green. But how could he abandon his father's latest invention? It wasn't even patented yet! Somebody could steal the idea and Dad wouldn't be able to do a thing about it!

At that moment, a sea of hysterical green people and dogs began pouring out of the benching area into the arena. Their footfalls were frenzied, their screams terrified as if they were being chased by a horrible supernatural creature. And there it was, following in their wake — not a zombie army, but the Orchard Spritz-o-matic, looking like a cross between a moving garbage can and a space-age lawn sprinkler.

Family loyalty overcame Griffin. He broke through the fleeing crowd and tackled his father's invention. Green dye soaked his face and clothing as he held on for dear life, screaming, "Where's the off switch?"

Mindless of the green drenching, Melissa hurried over and cut power to the device.

When Griffin wiped the dye out of his eyes, the first thing he saw gladdened his heart. There stood Luthor, nicely stacked and only slightly stained. Dmitri was with him, leaning on crutches, his pinkie fully extended. Griffin sighed his relief. Luthor was safe. Nothing could distract the Doberman when he was under the influence of the Russian's magical digit.

And then a young girl's voice — distant, yet clear as a bell — rang out over the chaos.

"Luthor!"

29

The big Doberman's clipped ears, upright as per the breed standard, twitched once and stood even higher, as if they were about to launch off the top of his perfect head.

Pitch's astonished voice crackled through Griffin's walkie-talkie. "Hey, isn't that —?"

At the very highest entrance, Savannah Drysdale surveyed the huge arena, realizing how futile it was to try to spot one adored dog in such a crowd. But she had to try.

"Luthor — sweetie!"

Like twin lasers, the dog's dark eyes fixed on her. Savannah — *his* Savannah! He'd thought her lost forever, but she had come back for him!

Griffin could almost feel a jolt of electricity shoot through the air as Luthor acquired the target. Dmitri must have noticed it, too, because he raised the pinkie higher and said, "Stay."

Luthor did not stay. He took off like a cruise missile, navigating the shortest distance between himself and Savannah. A few judges and show officials tried to calm him down and ended up having to leap for their lives. People and dogs dove in all directions to get out of his path. One look into those eyes was enough to convince anybody that this Doberman was not stopping. If there had been a brick wall in the way, there was no question that he would have blasted right through it.

Luthor did not run up the concrete stairs. He flew over the seats, his pumping paws barely touching the chairbacks. Savannah saw him then, burst into tears, and opened her arms. It lent him wings.

Using the last row as a springboard, he launched himself at the girl — just as the green-speckled culprit in black made for the exit behind Savannah.

Crunch!

Luthor never even noticed the collision. A second later, he was in Savannah's arms, being kissed and hugged and wept over. So much had happened in the past weeks to Lex Luthor Savannah

Spritz-o-matic — such wild highs and terrible lows that it went beyond a canine brain's ability to make sense of it. *This* made sense. He was back with Savannah, and all was right with the world.

Griffin was the first team member to pound up to the big reunion, but Ben, Melissa, and a slightly woozy Logan were hot on his heels. Seconds later, Pitch arrived via a scoreboard access ladder.

Griffin looked from girl and dog to the green-splashed figure lying dazed on the cement walkway. "Mrs. Devlin?" he blurted, astounded to see that Xerxes' owner had been the culprit all along. "It was *you*?"

Her expression was pure poison. "You ought to be ashamed of yourself — trying to pass that big moose off as a Doberman. And everybody's fooled because they *want* to be fooled — because Mr. Wonderful Dmitri Trebezhov puts his seal of approval on the fraud! Can anybody fault me for trying to make the show fair?"

"Yeah, I can fault you," Griffin said angrily. "You put Dmitri in the hospital. And what about Electra? She got a broken tail because of you. She'll probably never show again."

Mrs. Devlin sat up, still angry and unrepentant. "My Xerxes is twice the champion Electra ever

239

was! And if the judges had seen that, none of this would have happened."

"Oh, so this is *our* fault," came a silky, sarcastic voice from behind Griffin.

Everyone wheeled. There stood Mr. Charles Mannering-Smythe, chairman of the Global Kennel Society.

"Ha — you're busted!" exclaimed Ben.

"That is putting it mildly," said Mannering-Smythe. "Xerxes is excused from competition. And we shall see what the authorities think of your activities." He turned to Griffin. "And I regret to inform you that Luthor is also excused."

"What?" Logan was outraged. "What for?"

The chairman raised his chin. "For leaving his handler, for running rampant through the arena, for using a spectator — even an evil one — as a speed bump. Need I go on?"

Dmitri came thumping up. Even hunched on his crutches, he towered over Mannering-Smythe. "What you know about dogs," he accused, "would fit through the eye of a needle without touching the sides."

The man was insulted. "You think he should be Best in Show after such behavior?"

"I think he should be Best in Show *because* of such behavior!" the Russian thundered. "A good dog follows his training. But it takes a *great* dog to overcome that training for something more important than all the dog shows in the world."

"And what would that be?" sniffed Mannering-Smythe.

Dmitri gestured a crutch toward Savannah and Luthor, who were blissfully unaware of their surroundings. "Love," he replied. "True love. No blue ribbon could be a substitute."

Griffin was dismayed. "But we *need* that blue ribbon — not the ribbon itself, but the money that comes with it! We have to pay off the Drysdales' lawsuit so Savannah can keep Luthor! That's what the whole plan was for!"

"There will be no lawsuit —" A new voice rang out behind them. "Not against the Drysdales, anyway."

The group turned. They did not recognize the man, but at the end of his leash wagged the most famous bent tail in Dogdom. Electra.

"After what I've heard today," the beagle's owner went on, "I realize that Luthor is an innocent victim as much as my poor Electra. It is

Mercedes Devlin who will be hearing from my lawyers."

Savannah hugged her beloved dog and faced Griffin. "I'll be grateful to you my whole life for what you did for me and Luthor!"

Griffin flushed, embarrassed. "Don't forget the rest of the team."

"I'm not forgetting anybody," she replied. "But I know where the plan came from. And this was the greatest of them all. It was perfect in every way."

At that moment, a uniformed policeman burst in through the exit and boomed through an electric bullhorn: *"Attention, please! This is the NYPD. The building is under lockdown! We have reason to believe that a stolen Spritz-a-whosis is being held on the premises!"*

Mr. and Mrs. Bing came running up behind him.

"That's Spritz-o-matic!" the inventor corrected.

Griffin scrambled forward. "No, Dad — it's not stolen! It's right down there! And you'll never believe this — it *works*!"

30

For the first time in its illustrious 136-year history, the Global Kennel Society postponed its main event due to green slime. All the Best in Show contenders — not to mention dozens of other dogs, handlers, owners, judges, officials, spectators, and arena employees — had been splattered by the Spritz-o-matic's powerful jets. Luckily, the dye turned out to be easily washable, even from milk-white fur like Jasmine's. The next day, the seven finalists   including the replacement contenders from the working and toy groups — returned to the Coliseum to vie for the top prize.

The Bings, the Drysdales, and the team made the trip to New York for the judging. They were met at ringside by Dmitri Trebezhov himself. The legendary handler had decided to come out of retirement for good. He wasn't returning to Global, though. He was forming his own alternative dog show — one where dogs were encouraged to be free and express themselves.

The new show already had its first contestant. Savannah had signed up Luthor. "We're *so* going to win," she predicted as the Doberman watched the judging with great interest, his best friend, Cleopatra, perched contentedly on his shoulders. "Who's better at being himself than Luthor?"

Dmitri thought he had an answer to that question. Yesterday, he had filed the paperwork to adopt Xerxes. Technically, the Yorkie still belonged to Mercedes Devlin. But since she was under arrest and facing several counts of assault and malicious mischief, Xerxes would need a new master, and soon. Mrs. Devlin would probably receive prison time for what she did to Dmitri, Luthor, and Electra. At minimum, she would be banned from ever owning a dog again.

"Xerxes?" Ben repeated in distaste. "How can you go from a player like Luthor to a little rodent like him?"

Dmitri peered down at the small, slight boy.

"My undersized friend, you of all people should appreciate that great power often comes in small packages. Xerxes may look like a lapdog to you, but inside my miniature brother, I smell the heart of a lion. And Dmitri's nose is never wrong."

The contingent from Cedarville cheered the loudest when Jasmine was selected Best in Show. Luthor puffed up with pride as his "girlfriend" was draped with the winner's sash.

The only discouraging word came from Logan. "Showoff," he mumbled as the poodle preened with her big blue ribbon.

Pitch looked at him pityingly. "I know you. You're still bummed that your Manchurian weasel terrier wasn't allowed in. I've got news for you. He isn't even a dog. He's a ferret."

"And he isn't even *your* ferret," Ben added.

"I know that," Logan admitted frostily. "But a true actor can't just come out of a role overnight. It takes weeks."

When Griffin finally had the chance to congratulate Emma, he was humble and embarrassed. "I'm so sorry I accused you and your mom. I feel like a real idiot."

"You *are* a real idiot," she said with a dazzling smile. "But you're also a good person. Savannah told me everything you did for Luthor. That was awesome." Then, in front of the entire Manhattan Coliseum, the winning handler at Global wrapped her arms around Griffin and kissed him.

The Man With The Plan had seen his schemes pay off in many wonderful and unexpected ways. But never before had he been as pleased with a result as he was with Operation Doggie Rehab. For the better part of a week, his cheeks would remain a beaming red.

"*I'm* an idiot, too," she told him, shamefaced. "I was a total snob when I first saw Luthor. He's an amazing dog. And if he'd been out there today, he probably would have walked off with Jazzy's ribbon."

Although he'd been disqualified, Luthor was every bit the celebrity that Jasmine was on this day. He was also the #1 video on YouTube. Someone in the arena had filmed his bull run across the Coliseum yesterday. As he'd galloped toward his joyful reunion, several dogs had followed in his wake. Even the greyhound — right up there with the cheetah and pronghorn antelope on the list of fastest land animals — had been unable to keep pace with the big Doberman once Savannah was in his sights. It was easy to believe that a cheetah would have fared no better. Nothing could have outrun Luthor at that moment, not even a rocket.

Griffin had one more apology to give, this one to his parents. "I know I promised that there wasn't going to be any funny stuff while you guys were in Europe. I guess I messed up again."

Mr. Bing put a sympathetic arm around his son. "Well, I suppose there was a *little* plan. . . ."

"Little!" Griffin echoed ruefully. "It was the biggest of them all! The craziest, the most impossible —"

"Yes," his father agreed painfully. "But as a result of it, my Spritz-o-matic works. And *that's* what's saving your life."

"Besides," Mrs. Bing chimed in. "We may take issue with your methods, but no one could argue about what you did for Luthor. Look what a beautiful, well-behaved dog he's turned into."

Griffin nodded. He couldn't help wondering if Luthor would eventually unlearn all the training he'd received from Dmitri. In the end, though, it didn't really matter. In Griffin's mind, the Doberman would forever be standing ramrod straight, perfectly stacked, his coat gleaming in the spotlight of the dog world's brightest stage.

To The Man With The Plan, Luthor would always be Best in Show.